Dear John / Hank,

MEATBALLS AND MAYHEM & OTHER MYSTERIES

Thank you so much for your devotion to my grandmother. I know she loved you like a son.

I hope you enjoy this book. Look for "elsa" on pages 29-30.

Thank you,
Dawn

Dawn Rigney Geibel

Special Thanks:

To my husband Charlie for his loving support and encouragement;
To my three sons, Vic, Chris and Patrick, for answering countless questions;
To my father, Peter H. Rigney, for inspiring me with his writing, humor, and endless storytelling; and,
To author and teacher Angela Pisaturo, for giving me the push I needed to complete this book.

CONTENTS

MEATBALLS AND MAYHEM

MEATBALLS AND MAYHEM

Dana Runyon's perfectly good Monday morning was ruined by two things, a visit to the bank by cranky old Mrs. Henderson, and a phone call from Charlie, her husband of two years. First Mrs. Henderson came to the bank with a sack full of coins, which she had not counted, and poured them on Dana's desk. When Dana patiently explained the coins needed to be wrapped, Mrs. Henderson insisted on speaking with the bank manager. Even though it was against bank policy, Mr. Bradley smiled at Mrs. Henderson and told her Dana would be happy to count and roll the coins for her. Mrs. Henderson was after all a good, and not to mention wealthy, customer. Mrs. Henderson sat by and watched Dana count over two hundred dollars in small change with a smug expression on her face.

When Dana finished that task, she noticed the message light on her phone was blinking. It was a message from Charlie, letting her know their realtor, Carole Sinclair, had found them the "perfect" house. Thoroughly agitated, Dana ran her fingers through her blond hair, and pulled her navy blue cardigan tighter around her slender body. She knew Charlie was right, they did need to find a bigger house, but she was definitely starting to feel pressured. She met Charlie Runyon, a handsome, dark-eyed, local landscaper when she hired him to work on her yard. Marrying Dana was a package deal, with her three boys, and Annie, her tiny tuxedo cat, but Charlie didn't seem to mind. When he and his dog Sandy, a large Doberman-Shepherd mix, moved in, her house had become a little crowded. The charming three-bedroom house in Sea Cove, New Jersey had been her home in the years after her divorce from her first husband, and she hesitated to give it up. Was she just being selfish, as Charlie had mentioned more than once, or did she just want to hold onto a little of her independence?

When Dana called Charlie back he said, "It sounds perfect. The boys won't have to change schools and it is much closer to my job. There's a big yard with plenty of room for a garden, a front porch like you have always wanted, and best of all, four bedrooms and three bathrooms!"

Dana admitted it sounded like a good fit for the family and agreed to bring the boys to meet with Charlie and Carole after work. Driving south for a short five miles, Dana watched the street signs for Peninsula Road, and made a left towards the bay. With the car windows rolled down, a salty breeze blew through the car, indicating their closeness to the water. Dana had lived in the Jersey Shore area all her life, but Charlie had moved there from Long Island only a few years before. Both of them loved their casual life on the coast with its, beaches, seafood restaurants and pier attractions. Dana had not realized the house Charlie wanted to buy was this close to the water, and since she loved the beach, this was another selling point.

Charlie and Carole had their heads together discussing something and pulled apart when Dana and the boys drove up. Charlie came over to meet her as she got out of her car. *It's a good thing*

I am crazy about this woman, thought Charlie as he recognized the tight set to Dana's lips, and her narrowed eyes.

"What's going on?' Dana asked suspiciously.

"What do you mean, honey?" questioned Charlie, as he leaned over to give her a welcoming kiss. "We were just discussing closing costs, financing, you know, stuff like that." Seeing that Dana was still skeptical, Charlie added, "If you must know, I was telling Carole you might be a hard sell, that you were not so thrilled about the thought of selling your little house."

Bristling at the words "little house", Dana said, "Alright, I will try to be more open minded about all of this, but the house better be *perfect!*" Looking around she had to admit the yard was lovely, with a well-tended lawn, and flower beds that would need only a little work. There was a swing on the front porch, and without too much effort Dana could picture herself sitting there on a warm summer evening sipping iced tea. The boys could not wait and ran ahead to look inside the house. They were all hoping to have their own rooms, since their present house was a little cramped. Inside the house, Charlie and Carole were enthusiastically moving from room to room, but Dana held back. Something felt wrong, but she could not quite put her finger on what was bothering her.

As far as Dana could see, the house would be perfect, with plenty of room, extra bathrooms and closets. The house was a two story, with all four bedrooms upstairs. Downstairs was a living room, dining room, and family room that could be used for guests because of the French doors that could close it off from the dining room. The front porch was built totally across the front and down one side of the house. Two full bathrooms were upstairs; one half- bath was downstairs, as well as a half-bath in the double garage. Charlie was really excited about having a double garage; somewhere he could put his wood shop. In recent years he had started re-finishing furniture, but had no room for his tools in Dana's small garage. Through the back window, Dana spied a beautiful potting shed in the back yard, which had been built to look like a miniature version of the main house. *Just lovely,* she thought. Surrounding the yard was a privacy fence making this house harder to resist. There was a wooded area behind the fence at the back, and only one neighboring house was visible on the bay side. The few homes in the neighborhood had plenty of property, unlike their home now, where they were so close to the house next door, they could hear them talking at dinner through the kitchen window. One nagging thought running through Dana's head was the price of the house. It seemed a little low and Dana questioned Carole on how long the house had been on the market. Was is her imagination, or did Carole look uncomfortable?

"The house has been on the market for about eight months," stated Carole. "The last owners left suddenly and just wanted to get back the money they invested."

Charlie hissed in Dana's ear, "Try not to look for problems that are not there!"

"I'm not," insisted Dana. "This just seems too good to be true." Charlie and Dana promised to talk it over and give Carole their answer within a few days. Dana wanted one last look at the kitchen and was checking out the counter space and the cabinets when she detected a strange odor. *What is that?* she wondered. *Meatballs, I definitely smell meatballs!*

"Charlie, Carole, could you both please come into the kitchen?" Dana called. "I want you both to smell something!"

"What are you smelling, honey?" asked Charlie. "I don't smell anything."

"Me either." stated Carole.

"Don't you smell meatballs? Come over by the stove, the smell is stronger here."

Charlie and Carole just shook their heads.

"I think you are just hungry. How about going out for a pizza on the way home," suggested Charlie.

6

Dana started laughing. She probably was just imagining things, and she *was* hungry. As they all walked down the porch steps towards their cars, Dana did not notice Carole nervously looking back towards the house.

At their favorite little Italian restaurant, Villa Milano, Dana, Charlie and the boys weighed the pros and cons about the house while devouring two pizzas, an antipasto, and spumoni for dessert. The price of the house was amazing and everyone thought the location was perfect. Even better, it had the space they needed. Dana later realized she had let Charlie's enthusiasm cloud her judgment.

The discussion regarding the house continued in the car after leaving the restaurant. Vic, the oldest at sixteen, was especially in favor. His girlfriend Kim lived only a block away from the new house, and his best friend Lee also lived nearby. Vic was in a garage band, and he shook his long dark blond hair emphatically to make a point.

"We could practice more if I lived closer to Lee," he was saying.

Great, Dana thought. *Noise from the band all day Saturday was now going to include week nights also!* But instead of objecting, she just smiled and said, "We'll see", which the boys knew unfortunately meant "no" most of the time.

Vic also loved to cook and this kitchen was much bigger than the kitchen in their present house. He offered to cook at least one meal a week to give Dana a break if they moved.

His enthusiasm was spreading to the other boys as Chris added, "I wouldn't have to share a room with anyone!" As the middle child at fourteen, he was always the one who did not have his own room. The age gap between the oldest and youngest was too great for them to share, so Chris always had the choice of sharing a room with his older or younger brother. Chris, the most gregarious of the three, was blessed with blue eyes and wavy brown hair. He attracted lots of friends, both male and female. Having his own room would be an advantage for him as he always had someone visiting, and having either an older brother, or pesky younger brother hanging out with them was getting annoying.

Next Patrick spoke up. At ten years old, he was the youngest, so most of the time his brothers did not pay him any attention just to aggravate him. This time they listened. They knew being the baby of the family had its advantages and he might be able to sway Dana towards their point of view.

"Mom," he said sincerely, his dark eyes pleading, "this house is closer to the Youth Group Center. You would not have to drive me."

Oh brother, using the Youth Group angle. The kid was good!

Dana again replied, "We'll see." But the boys could sense she was weakening.

Once back home, the boys turned to Charlie, who had been their biggest ally since marrying their mother. Where Dana was strict, Charlie was more likely to give in. They each knew Charlie wanted to move because he had been very vocal about the subject for the past several months. Since his dog Sandy had been banished to the garage after eating two pairs of Dana's shoes, they knew Charlie was particularly eager to have a larger place with room for Sandy, and a large backyard where she could run.

Charlie winked at the boys and said, "Your mother and I will discuss this. I'm sure she will agree that this is the best move for everyone."

"Hmm, no pressure here!" Dana laughed. But she felt a twinge of annoyance because Charlie knew she did not want to move. Being an only child, Charlie was used to getting his way, and she knew he would keep pressuring her until she agreed.

By the next evening, when Dana had still not agreed, Charlie threw out his trump card. "If we buy a larger home, my kids Robert and Donna will have a place to stay when they come up North to visit." They both lived in Florida with their mother, and Dana knew Charlie missed them terribly.

"Well they both could visit for longer periods of time if there was more room," Dana admitted.

Finally Charlie offered what he knew Dana wanted most. "You could even work part-time if we move. When we sell your house, we could put all the money on the new house, and the mortgage payment will be smaller. With my landscaping company doing so well, I won't need your salary to help pay the mortgage."

Reluctantly Dana saw the benefits of the move, and told Charlie she would sell her house. Charlie's big smile and warm bear hug would have been enough for most women to know they had done the right thing.

"I'll call Carole in the morning," stated Charlie. "Should we wake the boys with the news?"

"No." Dana sleepily stated. "Let's wait until morning. If we tell them tonight, there will be no sleep for anyone. I'll tell you what, why don't you go tell Sandy?" She playfully punched him in the arm. "I'm pretty sure it's your turn to walk her anyway."

"I can't wait until we are in the new house. All I'll have to do is open the back door. No more of these late night walks!"

Dana was laughing as Charlie left the room. As she drifted off to sleep, a nagging thought kept trying to surface, but she just could not bring it up. What was bothering her? Oh well, whatever it is, it must not be that important.

⟩⊦ ⊦⟨

Three months later the family had packed and moved to the house on Peninsula Road. Dana and Charlie had been able to sell the Beechwood Drive house to an older couple almost immediately, and Dana marveled at how everything just fell into place. She had all but forgotten about her earlier reservations when she saw how happy Charlie and the boys were. Of course there had been the usual arguments as they were settling in.

"I don't want the middle room," stated Chris. "Just because I am the middle brother, does not mean I have to get the middle room! I want the one at the front of the house so I can see my friends coming up the street!"

Vic countered with, "I'm the oldest, I should get the first choice, and the biggest room, right Mom?"

Patrick, almost always agreeable asked, "Why do I always have to pick last?"

Ooh boy, I don't want to get into the middle of this one.

"Charlie," Dana called sweetly. "Can you come here and help with this dilemma? This move was your idea, so maybe you can solve this problem."

Charlie looked daggers at her as they passed in the hallway, and Dana was laughing by the time she reached the master bedroom.

"How many times will I be able to use *that* line before Charlie catches on?" she wondered out loud, as she entered the bedroom she shared with Charlie, and her little cat Annie, who liked to sleep with them to get away from Charlie's dog Sandy, who was always licking her head. The view from the master bedroom was lovely. Right outside the window were beautiful oak shade trees. A small park was across the street with winding paths and strategically placed park benches. She could see a basketball court where the boys could go shoot hoops, and she could go to the park for a morning jog, if she ever felt that ambitious. One of the boys would have the same view of the park, and the other two would look out over the large back yard. With Charlie's expertise in landscaping, she was sure the view of the back yard would be just as pretty in time.

Dana did not know how Charlie was able to do it, but the crises about the rooms had been settled. Chris would be in the front bedroom, and Vic and Patrick would be in the back. A long hallway adjoined all the bedrooms, with a bathroom in the middle for the boys. There was an oversized linen closet next to the bathroom, towards the back bedrooms. Dana was thrilled with all the new space and wondered if she even had enough towels and sheets to fill the closet. Pretty nice after years of cramming everything into too small spaces! Thank goodness the master bedroom had its own bathroom; Dana was tired of sharing one with the boys. No more toilet seats left up to surprise her in the middle of the night!

"I'm so happy, Charlie!"

"Me too! You'll see how wonderful life is going to be," Charlie smiled as he closed the bedroom door and took Dana in his arms.

"Who wants pancakes?' Dana called up the stairs early one Saturday morning. The noise of feet pounding down the wooden stairs answered her question.

"Do I smell bacon?" was the question from Vic. "Can I have some coffee?"

"Since when do you drink coffee?"

"Since Kim and I went to the Coffee Shack the other night."

"And just what is the Coffee Shack?" questioned Charlie, as he arrived last for breakfast, still looking rumpled and unshaven.

"All my friends go there." Vic stated. "We hang out and listen to music and try out different kinds of coffee."

"And you like the taste?"

Laughing Vic stated, "Not really, but Kim does. How about just giving me some pancakes and bacon? So, did you burn them this time, Mom?"

"You are so funny!" Dana stated, not really offended. After all, her cooking was really not that great. Even when she tried to follow the simplest recipe, the results were mediocre at best.

"So when do I get to collect on your offer to cook dinner, Vic?"

"Soon Mom, soon. Kim, Lee and I have something special planned. You'll just have to wait and see."

After everyone had finished eating, Dana cleared the breakfast dishes and thought about what to make for dinner that evening. Since she was finally able to cut down on the hours she worked, she found she was more organized and actually starting to enjoy cooking. Settling on a pasta dish, Dana was puzzled when she was unable to find her big sauce pot. Muttering, "Where did I put that pot?" Dana started going through all of the cabinets, with no luck.

"This is so strange; I thought I put that pot away yesterday. I must be getting absentminded. Okay, the pot must be in one of the boxes still sitting unpacked in the garage. And now I am talking to myself!" Dana decided to look for it later. She left the jar of spaghetti sauce on the counter and went upstairs to make beds.

A few hours later, Dana had finished her household chores and was once again in the kitchen. The counter-top was clean, and the jar of sauce was not in sight. She checked the refrigerator, and noticed the meat she left defrosting was also missing. Puzzled, she opened the freezer door and there it was, back on the top shelf. *I must be going crazy!* Once again she took out the meat. She opened the pantry and saw the sauce. Determined, Dana took the sauce out of the pantry and put it near the stove. She put the package of chop meat in the microwave on the defrost setting and turned it on. Now all she had to do was find her pots. The garage was just off the kitchen and Dana stepped out in search of the box she had marked, "Kitchen Stuff". Maybe the pots were there, though she swore Charlie had helped her unpack them the first day they moved in. She would have to ask him later.

Locating the box, Dana looked inside and gasped, "What happened to my sauce pot?" The inside looked all scratched and worn, and the larger pot she used to boil the water for spaghetti had a big dent.

"I can't believe the movers were this careless!" Dana wondered if it was worth filing a claim. She decided to wait and see if anything else was damaged. It was unlikely the moving company would pay off on such a small amount of damage. Still she was upset. Those pots had been a wedding gift from her mother. Dana never before had a set that matched, just a bunch of pots she picked up randomly, so these were really special to her. It was strange that she had not noticed any damage a few days ago. Lugging the entire box back to the kitchen, Dana smelled something burning.

"Oh, no!" The microwave was still running, and the meat had not only defrosted, it was cooked all the way through, and then some. There was no way she could make meatballs now. And where was that jar of sauce? Slowly Dana walked to the pantry, and there it was, back on the shelf.

"Ok, who is playing tricks on me? This is getting really old!" Dana paused and realized she was once again talking to herself, since no one else was home. Feeling like a fool she decided she must be getting absentminded. Maybe she pushed the wrong button on the microwave, and only thought she took out the sauce. Putting away her pots, Dana decided on macaroni and cheese, with a side of broccoli for dinner. Everyone liked that and there was little room for error. As she tossed the ruined chop meat into the garbage, Dana again detected a faint odor of meatballs. *Wishful thinking*, she laughed.

Heading back towards the stove, Dana noticed a mark on the faded old wallpaper above the stove.

"Hmm, that was not there before." The color resembled spaghetti sauce, and was very noticeable, especially on the wallpaper's small floral pattern "How on earth did that mark get there?"

Dana dragged the small kitchen step stool over to the stove, and tried to remove the mark with a sponge and a cleaning spray. No luck. The stain was not coming off the wallpaper. Well that was just one more thing to add to the growing list of work that needed to be done around the house. "Replace wallpaper", Dana wrote on the list she had hung on the refrigerator.

Later that night, with her family sitting around the dinner table, Dana recounted the day's events. She mentioned the possibility that the house might even be haunted. Charlie was skeptical, but her three children, having eaten Dana's cooking for many years, just laughed.

"Come on, Mom," said Vic. "This would not be the first time you burned dinner!"

Patrick came to Dana's defense. "Mom's cooking is okay. I think somebody was messing with her, probably you, Vic."

"Did not!"

"I'll bet!"

Charlie, trying to calm everyone down stated, "We all know Mom tries her best, but we do have pizza delivered more than any of my friends. Not that I'm complaining, but Dana, you may have just used the wrong setting on the microwave."

"Well," said Dana, "there was always that possibility, but there still seems to be something odd about this house."

"Not this old song and dance again," stated Charlie, exasperated.

"All right smart guy. Come in the kitchen with me and look at the wallpaper. You know I want it replaced, but you're too busy in your garden. Come see the new stain on the wall."

Everyone followed Dana to the kitchen where she pointed at a spot in the corner of the kitchen where the wallpaper exhibited a reddish oval spot.

"That was not there this morning, but it appeared after I opened the jar of spaghetti sauce."

Charlie looked at the spot and said, "Probably just some of the old wallpaper paste bleeding through. The steam coming up from the stove must have caused that."

"Do you really think that?" asked Dana. "Why can't any of you consider the possibility of a spirit dwelling in the house?"

"You mean a spaghetti stain ghost, Mom?" asked Chris.

The boys were laughing, at her no doubt, which only exasperated her further. Patrick started running the kitchen around saying, "Booooo." Sandy was chasing Patrick, barking furiously. Annie took refuge on the top of the stainless steel refrigerator.

"I don't believe in ghosts!" said Charlie. "Look, we'll pick out some new wallpaper this weekend and I will put it up on my day off."

"I don't think I want wallpaper. How about we strip off the old paper and paste, and paint the room white with one wall an accent color of bright yellow. I always wanted a kitchen that looked sunny. And with washable paint, any stains that show up can just be cleaned off."

Charlie agreed, and Dana was satisfied for now. Looking again at the spot, Dana swore it was now a little larger. *I must be overtired,* she thought.

"Okay, everybody out! I need to get the kitchen cleaned up. How about you go bring me the dinner dishes so I can load them into the dishwasher."

That was one luxury Dana really enjoyed in the new house. Her previous kitchen was small and had no room for a dishwasher, so she had to wash everything by hand. Dana did not like washing dishes any more than she liked cooking, and she always said she was bringing home takeout because she really did not have time to do dishes every night. Of course Dana knew the truth; she simply was a lousy cook!

In the next few weeks, Dana started noticing changes in her oldest son, Vic. At sixteen he had grown his hair long, and had dreams of becoming a rock star. The garage band he formed a few years before with his best friend Lee was doing well, performing at the local fair, and school dances. They had quite a following, but Dana was worried that he was so focused on the group, he was neglecting everything else. That changed shortly after they moved into the new house. This morning Vic came downstairs early and started cooking breakfast for the family. His long hair was combed straight back and fastened in a neat ponytail. Gone were his torn jeans and grubby t-shirt, replaced by his Sunday church clothes. Elegant leather loafers that Dana had never seen before replaced his unlaced Nikes.

Puzzled, Dana asked, "Where did you get those shoes?"

"They were on the top shelf of the linen closet. I found them there this morning when I was looking for a clean towel. Nice huh? Italian leather."

"I wonder if they were left here by the previous owners, though I don't remember seeing them when I unpacked and put the sheets and towels away."

"Well, they were there this morning, and my size, too!"

"Since when do you have such an interest in breakfast," Dana asked, yawning.

"Mom, you are always saying this is the most important meal of the day, right? Well, I found this amazing book on Italy on the bookshelf in the family room and started looking through the recipes. I think we should really start eating better!"

Dana exclaimed, "I can hardly get you to eat breakfast most mornings!"

"Well, that's about to change. Wait until you taste the bombolone I am about to bake. How about Cappuccinos for you and Charlie?"

"We don't have a Cappuccino maker."

"I think someone must have given you one for a wedding gift. I found it in the pantry."

"I don't remember getting a Cappuccino maker!" Dana exclaimed.

"Maybe it came from Aunt Helen." Vic added, "I'm going to make some hot chocolate for my brothers, too. And not the kind that comes from an envelope."

Dana yawned again. *This should be interesting.* She thought to herself. "I am going to go take a shower."

"Wait Mom. Do you mind if I make dinner tonight? And I'd like to have Kim and Lee come over, too. Since you are working today, I thought I would give you a break. I'll have Kim make the salad and Lee can make garlic bread."

"Really? Don't you guys just throw some frozen pizzas in the oven when I'm working late?"

"You know that stuff is not good for you, Mom. Too much sodium. That can't be good for Charlie's blood pressure."

Who was this kid?

Dana all but forgot about dinner because she was so busy at work. She had left money for Vic to purchase groceries for tonight's dinner, and was greeted by the aroma of something delicious cooking when she entered the house that night.

Kim and Lee were already there and Kim rushed over to give Dana a hug when she entered the kitchen.

"What a nice surprise to have all of you here cooking dinner," Dana said.

"Hi Mrs. G." Lee called from across the kitchen where he was slicing up a long loaf of bread to make the garlic bread.

Kim proudly pointed to a delicious looking salad she was making. Dana noticed black and green olives, cucumbers, tomatoes, celery, and Romaine lettuce all mixed together in one of her vintage blue Cinderella bowls, known for their spouts on both edges.

"Looks yummy!" she said to Kim, delighted that they were so enthusiastic about preparing this meal. "And just what does my number one son have cooking over on the stove. It smells wonderful."

"That must be the broccoli and green beans I have simmering with the sautéed garlic and crushed red pepper flakes. There are also potatoes baking in the over, and as soon as they are done

I am going to cut them in half and make twice baked potatoes. Mom, you are going to love the main course. I found this recipe for Steak Florentine, made with T-bone steaks. Really easy. I just added some kosher salt, a garlic rub, and salt and pepper. As soon as Charlie gets home I am going to cook them on your ridged cast iron skillet. The final touch will be to drizzle olive oil and squeeze a fresh lemon over the steaks."

Wow, was this my boy? Dana thought. She loved his enthusiasm, and just had to go over and give him a big hug, which thoroughly embarrassed him in front of his friends. Vic pushed her away and muttered something about needing to get back to cooking.

"Okay," stated Dana as she left the room. "I am going upstairs to get out of my work clothes. Call me if you need any help. Otherwise, I'll see you at dinner." She realized her stomach was growling. "Wow, I have never cooked anything that smelled that delicious."

Charlie came home a few minutes later. "What the heck is going on downstairs?" he asked. "I was not even allowed to get a yoo-hoo from the fridge. Whatever is going on, it smells delicious. So how much time do we have before dinner?" he asked, pulling Dana into his arms for a long kiss.

"Not *that* much time." she answered, laughing. Pushing him away she told him she'd give him a rain check on the romance. From the glint in his eye she knew he would be taking her up on the offer later that evening.

About twenty minutes later, Dana and Charlie were called downstairs for dinner. Patrick and Chris were already there, as Vic had enlisted them to set the dining room table. Charlie was told to sit at the head of the table, and Dana was seated opposite him at the other end. Linen napkins were placed by the dishes and Dana's crystal goblets were filled with ice and water. Tapered candles were lit at the center of the table, and soft music from stereo in the living room filled the room to complete the atmosphere.

"This is amazing, Vic." said Dana. Charlie agreed as everyone took their places at the table. Chris and Patrick were more interested in filling their stomachs than admiring the dinner, but they both agreed everything tasted delicious. Vic surprised everyone with a homemade gelato for dessert, tasting much like ice cream, but heavier, with a richer flavor. Kim and Lee were just as enthusiastic as Vic about cooking the meal. They talked about the fun the three of them had in Mrs. Bennett's third period cooking class, where they were encouraged to cook for their families to practice what they learned in class. Vic looked a little uncomfortable; he knew he never shared any of this information with his mother.

"I meant to tell you about this," he said. "I just never found the time."

"Uh huh. Well I am glad you are sharing with me now. And this meal was fantastic. You could show me some of the things you learned, and I could try out my cooking skills."

"What cooking skills?" asked Charlie.

"Funny man!"

"Maybe we'll come over and cook for you once a week." said Kim.

Charlie replied, just a little too enthusiastically, "That would be fantastic. Having a good home cooked meal would be great once in a while." Noticing the expression on Dana's face, Charlie amended his statement with, "Not that Dana is not a good cook, and she is just a little tired after work."

Dana could not help but laugh. Her culinary skills needed lots of work! Not only did she often order pizzas, but Chinese take-out was also a weekly staple!

After dinner, and over the objections of Vic, Kim and Lee, Charlie and Dana chased everyone out of the kitchen so they could do the dishes. Vic made Dana promise not to touch the cast iron skillet because he needed to properly season the pan. Dana promised, and the three teenagers went to Vic's room to listen to music.

"Wow, that was amazing," said Dana. "Who would have guessed that Vic was such a talented cook?"

"Yeah, I wonder where he got that ability." said Charlie.

"Enough cooking jokes!" said Dana, not really angry, just very proud of her son. They worked side by side in comfortable silence until the kitchen was sparkling clean again. Dana left the cast iron skillet on the stove as promised, happy not to mess with the heavy pan. Both wondered what Vic planned for next week.

⋙⧾⧽⋘

Dana was worried about Charlie. Mostly he went with the flow when it came to Vic, Chris and Patrick. As long as they didn't drink all of his yoo-hoos, he pretty much did not interfere with how Dana raised her children. Yet lately he was preoccupied with a garden he was trying to grow, and the boys seemed to aggravate him every time they came outside.

"What's the matter with Charlie?" Patrick had asked her this morning. Dana said she didn't know, but she was going to find out. Later she saw Charlie in the yard, sectioning off a small patch of earth with garden stakes and string. Charlie had planted marigolds all around the garden in the hopes this would keep Sandy from digging in the garden. Sandy was sitting nearby, happily munching on one of the marigolds. It was all Dana could do not to laugh, as she definitely did not want to aggravate Charlie further. She picked up several of the packets of seeds and read the names: Egg Plant, Plum Tomatoes and Sweet Basil. Hmmm, there was definitely a pattern here.

"So what's with all the Italian vegetables?" Dana asked.

"Vic can use them for his Italian cuisine," Charlie answered. "I'm just trying to get them growing as soon as possible. You know we only have spring and summer in New Jersey for planting. With my job I don't have as much time as I would like for gardening. I've started some as seedlings, but I bought tomato plants at the garden store. They are already flowering and some even have a few small tomatoes. Come over here and I'll show you what I've planted."

Charlie spent the next ten minutes showing Dana the rows of small sprouting plants, and explaining how tall each would grow, and when they could expect to have vegetables to eat, and herbs for use in cooking. Charlie had lots of theories on soil content, fertilization and acidity. He asked Dana to save the potato peel scraps, and leftover vegetables so he could make a compost pile. She saw a compost heap behind the garden that Charlie had already started.

"I'd like to build a grape arbor, too. Just think, if my grapes are delicious, in a few years I might be able to market my wine."

"Seriously? We don't have enough property for a vineyard! Where are you getting these crazy ideas?"

"I found some books on Italian herb gardens and wineries on the top shelf of the line closet."

"Really? Well maybe this is not the best time to get involved with a garden. We are still unpacking, and you promised to be an assistant coach on your friend Anthony's little league team. There's just so much time, Charlie."

"Stop being such a nag. You are always putting down my ideas, such as getting this house, and look how well that has turned out. Everyone seems happy, except you!"

"Well Patrick is not happy. You used to spend a lot of time with him, and now all your spare time is spent out here in your garden. Why don't you let him help you?"

"Because it is faster to do it myself. He has so many questions he just slows me down."

"He's only ten. Spending time with you is important to him now. In a few years he won't want to do that."

"Instead of complaining, why don't you and Patrick come out here and weed the garden during the week. Do you think the two of you can manage that?"

Dana, tears forming in the corner of her large green eyes, turned and walked back to the house. It seemed that Charlie only wanted to argue lately. Somehow moving to this house had not helped his disposition. *Maybe this move was not such a good idea.*

Entering the house, Dana once again detected the faint odor of meatballs. She wondered why no one else in the house ever noticed the odor. The smell alone had her craving Italian food.

＝⫸⫷＝

Dana was up early the next day making breakfast. She was getting a little tired of the Italian pastries and Cappuccino's. She had even put on a few pounds since Vic had started cooking in the morning. What she really craved today was scrambled eggs and toast. Dana made herself a cup of tea and was enjoying the quiet when Chris burst through the kitchen door, waving a piece a paper, which he handed to Dana.

"Bon Giorno, Mama. Please sign this for me."

Dana turned away from the breakfast she was cooking and said, "Wait a second, what is this?"

"It's your permission for me to drop out of my sixth period Spanish class and transfer to the Italian class."

"Why would you want to do that? Considering the direction this county is taking, you are going to find Spanish is going to be one of the most useful languages for you to have learned."

"I don't care, Mom. I just would rather study Italian."

"Just tell me why," said Dana, getting annoyed.

"Well for one thing, I'm part Italian. And I found an Italian phrase book and language tapes which will help me study."

"Let me guess, you found them in the linen closet."

"That's right, how did you know?"

"Oh, just a lucky guess. It seems there are lots of things in that linen closet. Everyone is finding something, except me." Reluctantly

Dana signed the permission slip, now more determined than ever to check out the linen closet. Maybe there was a secret panel?

Later that day, Chris came home from school all excited. He had been able to drop Spanish and add Italian to his classes. Dana was downstairs in the laundry room when she heard Chris calling her.

"Ciao Mama," said Chris. "I just learned that today. Do you know that 'Ciao' means hello or good-bye? Isn't that interesting? Italian is so much easier than Spanish. And guess what? Mrs. Bellini, my homeroom teacher, is also my Italian teacher. Isn't that great?"

Chris was never at a loss for words, either in English, or apparently in Italian. It was hard to find fault with his enthusiasm, and Dana only hoped that this would get Chris to study. He was very social and was always out with friends or talking to them on the phone. If he wasn't at home, he was visiting Clint or Eric. Recently he said he had a crush on Amber, a new girl in his homeroom. Dana was worried his grades would suffer as his popularity increased. So maybe this new interest in Italian would be a good thing, or so she hoped.

Later that evening, as Dana did her usual nightly check on each of the boys before turning in with Charlie, she heard talking coming from Chris' room. It sounded like Chris was watching television, which he was not allowed to do this late on a school night. Annoyed that he was still up, Dana opened Chris' bedroom door. Chris was in bed, asleep, but a cassette player was running on the nightstand next to his bed. From what Dana could hear, it sounded like Italian lessons.

This is getting ridiculous, she thought. Annoyed Dana walked across the room and turned off the recorder. Chris rolled over and mumbled, "Buono Notte."

"Good night to you too, young man," she said as she left the room. "We'll discuss this in the morning." Was it her imagination, or did Dana feel a chill in the air as she left Chris' room?

Early the next morning, Dana received the strangest request of all. Patrick came into the kitchen all excited before leaving for school. "Guess what I found in the linen closet?" he asked.

"I can't imagine," murmured Dana.

"A mandolin!" exclaimed Patrick.

"A mandolin?" Dana asked in disbelief.

"Yes. Isn't this great? And way cooler than the guitar. I want to switch my music class."

"Wait a minute, young man." stated Dana. "You have been taking guitar lessons for over a year now. Charlie and I bought you that guitar last Christmas. Mr. Nelson, your instructor, stated you have real potential and now you want to give that up to play the mandolin?"

"Come on Mom. At least let me try. I think I have always wanted to play the mandolin, but just did not realize it. Just think, I could play at church, and once people hear how great I am, I might even be asked to play at Italian weddings!"

"First of all," stated a very exasperated Dana, "You don't even know if you will be any good at playing the Mandolin. Secondly, why is everyone so obsessed in this house with being Italian? Don't forget, you are also half Irish."

"I know, I know. Who could forget when you make us all wear green on St. Patrick's Day! I just want to try this. It can't hurt to know how to play more than one instrument. Maybe Mr. Nelson can help me play this also. Please!"

Giving in, Dana agreed to let Patrick play a new instrument.

"I can't wait to hear what Mr. Nelson says when you show up with a mandolin for guitar practice."

"I'm sure he won't mind, especially when I tell him how it just showed up in the house. You may be right, Mom. Sometimes this house can be a little bit spooky."

"What do you mean, Patrick?"

"Well things just keep appearing, except there's nothing for you. Could it be the house does not like you?"

"How could a house not like someone?"

"I don't know, but everything nice happens to Charlie, Vic, Chris and me, and everything bad happens to you. Maybe you are right, Mom. The house could be haunted."

Dana, relieved that someone finally believed her, hugged Patrick tightly. "I am going to get to the bottom of this!"

Just then Vic came in the kitchen and noticed the mandolin in Patrick's hand.

"Cool. Where did you get that?"

"From the linen closet."

"Where else?" Dana muttered under her breath.

"You know you can't play that in my band, right?" asked Vic, knowing Patrick wanted to play with Vic's band when he got older.

"I don't care," said Patrick. "You just play at stupid fairs and school dances. I am going to make big bucks playing at Italian weddings!"

"What? You're crazy. No one hires mandolin players. Maybe you could move to Italy!"

"Mom! Vic is picking on me!"

"Okay, okay. It's too early for all this bickering."

What in the world was going on?

It was time to visit the linen closet. Something was definitely weird. Dana pulled open the double doors expecting to feel a blast of chilled air, or, at the very least, be assaulted by a putrid small. Nothing. She started to feel foolish. *I must be watching too many movies on the SYFY channel*, she thought. Standing on a small white stepstool she had carried upstairs from the kitchen,

Dana started taking towels off the top shelf, looking for a hidden compartment. Where could all the items Charlie and the boys found be coming from? She methodically emptied the entire linen closet and found absolutely nothing. Knocking on the walls inside the closet revealed no hollow sounds, and the closet proved to be just a normal linen closet. Except now she had a big mess on the floor where she had dumped the towels and sheets.

"Okay house, you win! You don't like me and I don't care," Dana said in frustration. *Great, I'm talking to the linen closet.* Dana laughed a shaky laugh and went to work putting everything back.

⊶⊷

As she had promised earlier in the week, Dana met her friend, Cathy, at the Corner Café for lunch. Quickly ordering pastrami on rye with a side of potato salad, the cafe's specialty, Dana said, "Cathy, I am so glad you invited me to lunch."

"Me too! I've really missed our lunches since you went part-time."

"I have so much to tell you, most of it unbelievable. Living in this new house has been so bizarre!"

"Bizarre? What do you mean?"

"It's a little hard to explain, so I want you to come over and experience what is happening for yourself. I've been learning how to cook, so would you like to come over for dinner?"

"Dana, you're cooking? That is bizarre. How did this happen?"

"Very funny, Cathy. This will sound crazy, but I feel that there is some sort of presence in the house, and that it wants me to be a better cook. Don't look at me like that, Cathy. I know it sounds crazy, but strange things happen when I cook badly."

Looking very skeptical, Cathy asked, "What kinds of things?"

"Well sometimes my pots and pans disappear, or they get dents in them. Or I put something on to simmer and when I come back in the room the burner is turned up high and the food is burned."

"That sounds like your cooking!"

"Seriously, other peculiar events are happening. Charlie and my kids all seemed to have developed different personalities. They also find very strange items in our linen closet. Please come over one Saturday night and let me know what you think."

Cathy laughed. "Sound interesting, I will try to make it. Can I bring something?"

"No, just come, I promise it will be worth it."

"Are you getting Chinese takeout?

"Everyone's a comic."

The two women hugged and promised to make dinner plans for later in the month.

After lunch with Cathy, Dana decided to pay a visit to Carole at Seaside Realty, hoping to get some background on the house. Dana parked her black sedan about a block away from the small storefront real estate office. Carole was on the phone when Dana walked into the office, and waved Dana to a seat in front of her desk, holding up her finger to indicate Dana was to wait a moment until Carole finished her call. While waiting, Dana glanced around the office, hoping to find a coffee pot. She thought she smelled fresh coffee brewing, which made her want a cup. She spotted the pot near the back of the office, and casually walked over and poured herself a cup in one of the Styrofoam cups stacked near the pot. She was pleasantly surprised to see flavored creamers, instead of that powdered junk that passes for milk.

The office was pretty much bare bones; linoleum floor, three in-expensive desks, office supply store stackable chairs lined up along the windows, and two in front of each desk for customers. Seemed like a lot of chairs for an office that was so empty. Dana could not remember if Carole had a partner, or any employees. She was fairly aggressive and seemed like she would be a difficult employer.

Dana studied Carole while she was talking. Charlie had told her he met Carole at a singles' dance years earlier, and Dana wondered if there had ever been anything between them. It did not seem likely as Carole was so abrasive, and Charlie liked to be in charge. It just seemed their personalities would clash.

Carole was finally off the phone, so Dana walked back over to the desk and sat down. "So, tell me about the house."

Carole would not meet her gaze. "What are you talking about?" she asked.

"Come on Carole, something is not quite right about that house and I think you know what it is."

"Well, the house does have a history, but that was a long time ago. I did not think it was even important enough to mention."

"Really?" asked Dana. "Why don't you "mention" it now? Why did the last owners move out?"

"Uh, they were not specific, but they talked about noises and odd smells. Nothing scary, but when they had the chance to move closer to their daughter in Connecticut, they decided to leave."

"It seems you should have disclosed this to us when you were showing us the house. Especially when I told you and Charlie that I smelled meatballs in the kitchen! So what is the history of the house, did something unusual happen there?"

Carole had the grace to look guilty as she admitted, "I think there was a murder in the house in the early 1950's, but I don't know much about it."

"A murder! How about you tell me what you **do** know, Carole."

Dana listened in shock as Carole filled her in about the history of the house. Carole did not have all the details, and told her what little she knew.

After a few curt words to Carole, Dana left the real estate office. It was only a few blocks to the Sea Cove Public Library, and she was hoping to get more information there.

⊷┼┾⊷

The Sea Cove Public Library was in small brick building off of Route 9, with long glass windows that overlooked a shaded courtyard. Dana saw local high school students sitting out on the benches, reading or talking. She was hoping the library, which had been built about the same time as the town, would have an archive section. Purposefully, she strode up to the desk to ask the librarian for help.

"Excuse me," Dana said, smiling as the librarian looked up from her computer. "Does this library have an archive section?"

"It most certainly does," replied the librarian, identified on her name tag only as "Ella".

This is great, thought Dana. *Ella certainly looks old and she might have some memory of the events surrounding our house.*

"Just what are you looking for? If you give me some information or a time period, it will certainly help me locate the information you are seeking."

"Well," said Dana, "my husband and I just bought a home on Peninsula Road just outside of town, near the beach. I understand it was vacant for a long while, so we were able to get a very good deal. Now I am hearing the reason the house remained vacant for so long was due to some mystery surrounding an old Italian couple that lived there for many years in the mid-century."

Ella looked thoughtful for a moment, absently tugging on a long piece of grey hair that had escaped the bun on the top of her head.

"Well dear, I think I can help you. I do remember rumors about a house where something tragic occurred many years ago. Let's go see if that is your house."

29

Leading Dana past several rows of bookcases, Ella turned and entered a small office near the back of the library. There were stacks of newspapers covering a timeworn desk, and a very old micro fiche machine. Dana commented she did not think those old machines were even being used today.

Ella laughed, stating, "It may be old, but it works, just like me. Someday we may have the funds to update our equipment, but for now this will have to do."

Dana sat in front of the micro fiche and Ella showed her how to locate the time period in question.

"I'll just leave you here to search for your information. If you need me, just come get me at the front desk. I'll be here until at least 4:30."

Gratefully Dana thanked Ella, and began the search for any information concerning a tragedy in the house. Carole had given her an approximate time frame. Painstakingly Dana pulled the old films through the viewer, reading about weddings, deaths, real estate transactions and numerous everyday occurrences of a small town. She knew the family name was DiNardo, and was encouraged when she came across an article about a high school graduation, listing an Anthony DiNardo, Jr., from 1942. Ok, she was at least in the correct timeframe. Still scrolling, she found an article about the wedding of a daughter, Grace, and another article about Anthony Jr., a few years later, when he graduated college. Nothing too exciting. Wait, here was something. The DiNardo's opened an Italian restaurant in the center of Sea Cove in 1945. An old picture showed Anthony and his wife, Nona, cutting the ribbon in front of a small brick building. The mayor of Sea Cove was there also, and everyone had big smiles on their faces. According to the article, Nona DiNardo was a renowned chef. Her specialty was Ziti and Meatballs, and she could be counted on to cook for every church social, if asked.

This looks like a happy group, thought Dana. *I wondered what could have happened.* Dana scrolled through several more years of film before the DiNardo's were mentioned again. This time the mention was of Mr. DiNardo's big gambling losses, and how they had to close the restaurant due to bankruptcy.

Could this have been the start of their troubles?

The lives of Anthony and Nona DiNardo worsened after that. There were documented public fights, drunkenness, and one last entry. Anthony DiNardo made one unforgiveable mistake. At a family dinner one Wednesday night, following Anthony's consumption of too much red wine, he criticized Nona DiNardo's cooking, especially her meatballs and sauce. This proved to be too much for Nona. He had lost their money, ruined their restaurant's reputation, embarrassed her in public, and she forgave him. But to criticize her cooking, that was too much. According to reports, Nona DiNardo calmly got up from the table, walked to the kitchen and came back with the big cast iron skillet she used to brown her meatballs. Anthony DiNardo had barely lit his big, smelly after dinner cigar when his wife came up behind him and, in front of Grace and Anthony, Jr., bashed him in the head with the skillet. One fatal blow was all it took. Then the horror of what she had done sunk in and Nona DiNardo had a heart attack and collapsed on the floor. She was dead before the ambulance arrived. Dana just sat in front of the microfiche machine in silence. How sad for the DiNardo's! Was it possible that was why Nona DiNardo was unable to rest?

Ok, thought Dana. *Maybe if I learn to cook, Nona DiNardo might just warm up to me a little bit.* Dana started laughing. She could not believe how absurd she was starting to behave! How could a long dead Italian woman have any influence on the events in her household? But just in case......!

Later that morning Dana headed north on the Garden State Parkway for a trip to the Ocean County Mall. She figured she could pick up a cookbook from the bookstore, and maybe do a little shopping on the same trip. That would be her reward for the arduous task of learning to be a better cook. Dana would be the first to admit that cooking was not high on her list of subjects to master. Not when there were so many restaurants willing to cook for her! And weren't the frozen selections getting better and better? Not like when Dana was a kid and there were maybe five different selections of TV Dinners that her step-mom kept stocked for Friday night dinners.

The store clerk at Shoreline Books directed Dana to the cookbook section. Having never bought a cookbook, Dana was amazed at the sheer number of books lining an entire aisle. Wasn't there just a simple Italian cookbook? After browsing through at least twenty Italian cookbooks from all different regions in Italy, Dana settled on *Italian Cooking for Beginners*. The recipes looked simple, with limited ingredients, and the preparation time on most of them was short.

Finished at the bookstore, Dana walked absently walked through the mall, wanting to get an outfit for the romantic dinner she and Charlie had planned for this week-end. She was hoping to rekindle a little romance in the marriage, if she could just get him out of the garden! After picking out what she hoped was a dress that would capture Charlie's attention, Dana left the mall and headed for the A&P Supermarket located on Route 9 near her home. Taking the cookbook with her into the store, Dana settled on a basic spaghetti sauce recipe, a simple meatball recipe, and the ingredients for garlic bread. Adding some fusilli, a crusty loaf of Italian bread, a head of lettuce, some ripe tomatoes, a cucumber, black olives, onion, garlic cloves, olive oil and red wine vinaigrette to her shopping cart, Dana felt ready to tackle her first simple home-cooked Italian meal. Now for dessert. A simple fruit salad with cannoli cream would complement the meal. Dana was pleased the cannoli cream was little more that ricotta cheese, whipping cream, powdered sugar and cinnamon. She planned to fill small bowls with strawberries, raspberries and cut up kiwi, and place a dollop of the ricotta cream on top, adding some toasted almonds for show. With these new ingredients in her shopping cart, Dana hurried to the checkout, anxious to go home and get started on her meal, noting the sauce, made from scratch, needed to be cooked for several hours.

Remembering her past failures at making spaghetti sauce in her new kitchen, Dana was a little apprehensive when she returned home and unpacked the groceries; she was anxious for this meal to be a success. She really did love Italian food, and was embarrassed that her sixteen year old son was a better cook than she. Dana only hoped the ghost of Nona DiNardo would cooperate. She was now convinced that all the mischief in the house had been caused by Nona. So as she laid her ingredients out on the speckled brown granite countertop, she began to speak aloud to her tormenter.

"I know why you don't like me. Cooking was very important to you and you think I don't show enough respect. I am going to try to do better and hope you help me by not moving my pots, or burning my sauce. I read about you in the *Sea Cove Gazette* and your culinary talent was well known in local church circles. Your husband did not give you the respect or praise you deserved, and he paid dearly for that."

Dana only hoped no one walked in on her while she was talking to Nona DiNardo through the dinner preparation. She knew she sounded crazy, but Dana really believed the ghost of the old woman was there in spirit, and was not going to give up her kitchen to Dana unless she felt Dana was worthy.

"Ok, here goes," said Dana as she browned some sausage, chopped onion and fresh sliced garlic in her large sauce pot. In a separate bowl, Dana combined ground chop meat, bread soaked in milk, eggs, parsley and spices. As she shaped the mixture into meatballs approximately two inches in diameter, she carefully dropped them one by one into the sauce pot with the cooked sausage and garlic, turning them as they browned until done. What a heavenly smell! Dana got a strong feeling of approval and felt acceptance in her kitchen for the first time. Dana took the meatballs and cooked sausage out of the pot, and prepared to make her sauce. Having received a tomato grinder as a wedding gift, she took it out of the closet and used it for the first time. Grinding the fresh tomatoes removed the seeds and pushed the tomato through the holes into the pot. She added some spices, some fresh basil, two bay leaves and chopped parsley, cooking wine and a pinch of sugar. As the sauce started to simmer, Dana added the meatballs and sausage to the mixture and set it to simmer.

"Please do not burn!" she pleaded.

Dana decided to cut the fruit and after adding some lemon juice and sugar, she placed the bowl of fruit to chill in the refrigerator. The Cannoli cream could be made just before the dessert was served. Knowing it would be a few hours before she would need to make the salad and prepare the fresh garlic bread, Dana decided to use the time to do some cleaning and throw in a load of laundry. She was very excited to surprise her family with this home cooked meal, and was amazed how satisfied this made her feel. She wasn't sure, but thought she felt a gentle pat on her back.

"Well, well Nona DiNardo, there you are. Thanks for stopping by. Please keep an eye on my sauce."

Dana was chuckling as she left the room, but she was only half joking. She really felt the presence of the old woman, and wondered if she was going to inhabit the house with them for years to come, or just until she was satisfied with Dana's progress in the kitchen.

Later that evening, dinner was a great success. Even Vic, who initially had asked if the meal was catered, was impressed.

For the next several weeks, Dana continued cooking meals for the family, using the recipes from her new cookbook. Her friend Cathy, who came by for dinner one week-end, complimented Dana's new cooking skills as well. Dana even unpacked a few cookbooks she had received as wedding gifts, but never bothered to open. Her most cherished cook book, however, was a well-worn volume, with notes scribbled in the margins, that Dana found one morning in the linen closet.

As Dana learned to cook, she started to notice subtle changes in the house. For the first time in a few weeks, Vic was not the first one in the kitchen. He came shuffling in after she got up, in a T-shirt and sweat pants, his hair disheveled.

"So Mom, do we have any cereal? How about some Lucky Charms?"

"What? You're eating a cereal with sugar? Seems like old times."

"I know it seems odd, but that's what I want."

Patrick came in next, lugging his guitar case.

"Mr. Nelson was not too enthusiastic about the mandolin, so I guess I will go back to the guitar. Besides, Sarah made fun of me."

"Sarah?"

"She's in my guitar class."

"Well, if Sarah made fun of you, I guess you need to stop the Mandolin lessons," Dana said, trying to hide a smile. *Thank you, Sarah!*

Chris entered with a big smile and a, "Good morning, Mom."

"What, no *Bon Giorno?*"

"Nah. Italian is too hard. Could you sign this note for my transfer back to Spanish class? Mrs. Bellini said I could come back and she would help me catch up."

Charlie was last up that morning. He came in and gave her a big bear hug and said, "How about you and I take a trip to the local Farmer's Market next Saturday. My garden does not look too healthy and I am thinking of turning it under and replacing it with a badminton court for all of us. I bet we can beat the boys."

"Not a chance," said Vic, laughing.

Dana, happy to have her family back, walked outside with them as they each left for school, or in Charlie's case, work. Annie, who was finally warming up to Charlie, was winding around her feet, looking for attention. Had Dana turned around at the exact moment she kissed Charlie good-bye, she would have seen a shadowy figure in her bedroom window, an old Italian woman with a satisfied smile on her face, disappearing into the shadows.

THE ACCIDENT

THE ACCIDENT

The accident wasn't her fault; everyone told Susan the same thing. Not that it mattered, Edward was still dead. How many times had she wished she had not taken the wheel of the car that rainy night?

"I'll drive." She told Edward in anger. "You are much too drunk."

At the party Edward also was too flirtatious with Celia, Michael's wife, and too loud, and too, well just too "everything". They fought as they drove off from the party, and Edward just laughed in her face at every accusation she threw out. Susan and Edward had seemed like an ideal couple five years ago when they wed. They both loved sports, they enjoyed dancing and dining out. Spending weekends checking out antique stores to furnish the ten room mansion Edward's parents had purchased for them as a wedding gift was also a shared passion. Lately though, Edward seemed to enjoy embarrassing her in front of their friends. He would leave her sitting alone during an evening of dining and dancing while he asked all of his business partner's wives to dance. For the most part the men were relieved to have someone else entertain their wives while they sat and discussed upcoming sports events or talked business.

"Who is going to dance with Emily and Celia if I don't?" he would ask her.

"Well I like to dance, too." Susan would protest.

When Edward stated he just did not care, Susan held back angry tears. Tonight Edward was more blatantly flirtatious than usual. Having endured enough, Susan reached over to slap Edward's face just as the car hit an icy patch, skidded across the road and smashed into the chain link fence that kept old Mr. Bell's cows from wandering off his property. Edward had stubbornly refused to wear his seatbelt and was thrown headfirst into the windshield. He died a few hours later at Meadowview Hospital from massive head trauma. Susan remembered thinking that "Meadowview" was much too lovely a name for such an ugly event. Her last memory of Edward alive was him being loaded into the county ambulance.

The funeral was a nightmare. *I am sorry for your loss.* Susan heard that phrase a hundred times throughout the memorial service, except from Edward's parents, who kept an icy distance throughout. At the very end, Edward's mother came over to Susan and stunned her with this revelation.

"Edward no longer loved you, Susan. He told me he was going to ask for a divorce. All that money you are going to get from his estate should never go to you. Maybe you found out and murdered him!" Susan was too shocked to reply.

In the weeks that followed, Susan packed up Edward's belongings and sent some of his personal items to his parents. She realized Edward's mother had spoken the truth when she found hotel receipts, telephone numbers and other evidence Edward had not been faithful in the pockets of his expensive suits. How could she have been so blind? Apparently she ignored some very obvious indications.

When a tearful and angry Susan confided all she had discovered to her best friend Janis, she was shocked that Janis was not surprised.

"Susan, you had to know what a flirt Edward was," said Janis. "He even came on to me a few times."

"Why didn't you tell me?"

"Would you have believed me?"

"Honestly, I don't know. But at least I would have been watching for signs of his infidelity."

"And then what. A lengthy drawn out divorce? Didn't you sign a pre-nuptial agreement with Edward before the wedding?"

"Yes. Edward's parents were insistent. If I had divorced him I would have been left almost penniless. Edward's death left me well off financially. The money in all our accounts goes to me, as well as the cars and jewelry Edward gave me before and during our marriage. Only my engagement ring, which belonged to Edward's grandmother, remains in his family. I have already given it back to his mother. She practically yanked it off my finger at Edward's Memorial Service. Once the house is sold, half the money goes to me, and half to his parents, as they stipulated when they made the purchase for us before the wedding. If Edward had thought to make a Will, all of this might have been different. Of course you always think you are too young to die.

"So maybe this is for the best," said Janis. You have all the money you need, and no longer have a lying, cheating husband."

"Janis! What a thing to say!"

"Well most of the women we know are thinking the same thing, believe me," answered Janis.

Susan had plenty of time to reflect on Janis' words. Edward had left her a great deal of money, much of it from the life insurance policy he purchased right after their marriage. First Susan quit her job, and then she gave away the rest of Edward's belongings to the local Salvation Army, much to the horror of his parents. With the house up for sale, Susan had to decide what to do with her life. Travel? Charity work? Classes at the local college? All very real possibilities.

Susan's first course of action was to plan an extended vacation. Packing for a two week Mediterranean cruise, Susan hoped the diversion would help to ease the pain of Edward's betrayal and death, especially since she decided bring Marco, her sexy new gardener, as her guest.

DEADLY SEAWEED

DEADLY SEAWEED

"Hey Rachel, get a move on," yelled Todd from the kitchen. Rachel groaned and turned over to go back to sleep. Todd came into the motel's bedroom and shook Rachel to get her up and moving.

"Darcy and Robbie are already outside securing the Kayaks into the bed of the truck."

The four friends had driven down to Florida from Tennessee yesterday in Todd's large red Ford 150 pickup, which not only had a large truck bed, but also a double cab so all four of them could fit inside for the trip. They were staying at a small motel on Tarpon Avenue, a street populated by restaurants and antique shops, and just a few short miles from the Gulf of Mexico.

"Dan's Kayak Rental delivered them just as promised a little after 8:30," Todd continued. "You are the only holdup. Were you up late doing more research on seaweed?"

"Okay, okay. I'm getting up, and yes, I was doing research late last night. That is the reason for my trip, remember. My thesis is on the effects of seaweed on area beaches and you guys wanted to tag along."

"True, true, but try to have some fun." Todd leaned over to kiss Rachel's cheek and then dropped a pair of shorts and a T-shirt over her still motionless form. "Put these on and meet us outside. There's some toast and coffee waiting for you in the kitchenette."

Brushing her teeth, running a comb through her long streaked blond hair and securing it with a rubber band into a messy pony-tail took just a few minutes. Running out the door with the toast in one hand and a coffee mug in the other, Rachel's breath was taken away by the oppressive heat.

"Well thank God we will be out on the water today. I don't think I could stand too much of this heat," she said to no one in particular.

Rachel grew up in Florida, but had spent the last several years in college in Tennessee. As each season changed to the next, Rachel was drawn in by the glorious red and gold colors of the fall, the softly falling snow in winter, the emerging blossoms in spring, and finally the summer, the heat so familiar to a Florida girl. Remembering the Florida weather is what drew Rachel to this project. Living in Tarpon Springs for most of her life, she was surrounded by water, and a lot of her time was spent on the area beaches which she loved, except for the massive amounts of seaweed in the water, and washed up on the shoreline.

The humidity curled Rachel's hair into damp ringlets which refused to stay caught up in her pony tail. The high humidity was adding about ten degrees to an already hot day. In Florida, the heat index was more accurate than the actual temperature.

"Okay," called Rachel, "We're going to be out on the water for several hours today. Have you packed water, snacks, and most important of all, sun tan lotion?"

"Yes Mom," replied Darcy, with just a hint of sarcasm. She came along on this trip because Robbie had asked her, but she was only interested in a great tan and maybe some recreational romance.

The drive to Sunset Beach took less than ten minutes. Bumping along the sandy dirt road towards the beach, heat and dust washed over them. The sand was largely unoccupied, except for a small flock of sea gulls, patiently standing around waiting for fiddler crabs to emerge from their small holes in the sand to provide an easy breakfast. Watching with mistrust as the large pickup parked close to the sand, the birds leisurely strolled a little further down the beach.

While Todd and Robbie untied the bright blue and yellow Kayaks and dragged them out to the beach, Darcy unloaded the supplies. Surprised by the amount of seaweed on the beach, Rachel headed down with a cooler and collected samples from the massive piles which had apparently washed up overnight. There was double the amount on the shore this morning than she had seen the previous evening when she had come for a quick look just before sunset. A strange smell emanated from the seaweed, almost pungent. The sand, normally dry and gritty this time of day, was still damp under the seaweed.

"Look at this, guys," Rachel called over her shoulder. "This seaweed looks almost alive, not with the crisp, dry texture I was expecting. It's still pliant and moist."

"So what." said Darcy. "You can squat down here and examine the disgusting seaweed all day, if you want. Me? I'm going kayaking with the guys. We only have the kayaks for three days, and I plan to make the most of that time."

"I think it's beautiful, and interesting," Rachel added, ignoring Darcy's sarcasm. "First I need to get my samples, and then I'll join you. I have to compare the beach samples to the seaweed in the gulf."

Looking out over the water, there seemed to be more seaweed than usual floating along the shoreline. Rachel noticed large clumps almost obliterating the surface of the beautiful blue-green water of the Gulf. Concerned, Rachel walked to the water's edge.

"I've never seen the seaweed this heavy before."

"I agree with Darcy. The seaweed is pretty disgusting," agreed Todd. "But we should paddle past it in a few minutes."

"I don't know, it seems to go out pretty far. You guys head out towards the island and I'll come along right after I put my samples in the cooler. I hope I have enough ice packs to keep the seaweed fresh until we get back to the motel later this evening. I'll get the rest of the samples as I paddle on the water, and also some from the island. I should be able to fit twenty-four of the wet-stack liquid vials into the cooler. Tomorrow I will bring a new cooler for more samples. Go ahead. I promise I am right behind you."

Reluctant to leave Rachel behind, Todd finally agreed and joined Robbie and Darcy at the water's edge. Placing their fully loaded backpacks in the canoes, the trio waded into the water, which was shallow for at least fifteen yards out. The seaweed made visibility to the bottom of the gulf water impossible and Darcy was disgusted by the muddy bottom she had to walk through.

"Yuck! I'm getting into the kayak. You guys can walk through this muck if you want." She liked that she was able to sit entirely on the surface of her kayak. She was afraid of the ones where only your body was on top and your legs were in the cavity of the kayak. If she was to turn over, she was positive she would drown. Plus, she had great legs and was very happy displaying herself on the top of the canoe in a very tiny bikini. Todd and Robbie finally got in their Kayaks and all three started paddling to a small island they could just see in the distance. Rachel was now pushing off shore and struggled to catch up with her three friends.

"Wow, I can barely paddle. The seaweed is so heavy I have to stop every few minutes to wipe the plants off the blades. How are the rest of you doing?" Darcy, Robbie and Todd were all having the same problem.

"At this rate it will take hours to get out to the island," complained Darcy.

"No, the water looks clearer not too far from here," said Robbie. "Just a little farther." He paddled up along-side Darcy's Kayak to offer encouragement. He liked Darcy a lot and hoped to get to know her better on this trip.

Todd held back and watched Rachel coming towards him. He really liked Rachel, but she did not appear to be interested in anything more than slimy seaweed. Her progress was slow as she pushed through the seaweed and collected samples from the water. Once they passed through all the dense seaweed, paddling was easier and they were able to enjoy the water. Everyone had slathered on suntan lotion of at least SPF50 at Rachel's encouragement, which partially protected them from the relentless sun in a cloudless blue sky. As the four paddled closer to shore, they noticed a circle of greenish brown surrounding the island. The seaweed was not as thick as it was back on the mainland, but it was still hard to get through as it stuck to the blades of their paddles. Rachel planned to collect a few more seaweed samples, but it was clear Darcy, Todd and Robbie were more interested in having a picnic and getting a nice deep tan. Rachel could not blame them. She was, after all, the only real nerd on the trip. But she did relax and enjoy the day, and for a little while she pushed aside her excitement of the possibility she had discovered a new species of seaweed. She planned to call Professor Thomas, her botany professor at college, just as soon as she was back at the motel.

The group played volley ball, swam in the few areas where there was very little seaweed, ate a picnic lunch, and mostly just enjoyed the sun and applying sunscreen to each other's toned bodies. That was Darcy's favorite activity. After spending several hours on the island, the group reluctantly packed up the kayaks and got ready for the short trip back to the mainland. Even Rachel admitted she had a great day.

Todd commented, "See Rachel, you do need to take a break once in a while."

The kayak trip back to the mainland was uneventful, except for once again paddling through thick seaweed. The beautiful sunset turned the gulf waters into the most stunning hues of red and gold. Even Darcy was impressed. On the way back to the motel, Rachel called Professor Thomas and left a message asking him to call.

Rachel kept most of the seaweed samples in jars filled with salt-water, but did bring in some of the stalks to attempt a seaweed salad, which she heard was a staple in some countries like Japan, China and Korea. Darcy thought that was a joke and suggested maybe they should put some in rolling paper and smoke it instead. Darcy had quite a reputation at school for being a "party girl". She did just enough work to pass her courses and hoped to marry well, and do as little work as possible.

Rachel explained seaweed was fat free and loaded with vitamins and minerals, one of the richest sources of both in the vegetable kingdom. Plus its nutrients could feed the shafts and ducts of the human scalp, which would improve the health of hair. Rachel had read somewhere during her extensive research that the Japanese owe their thick, dark hair in part to the consumption of seaweed, though she was not sure how much of that was true. It was almost a "perfect food".

Even while Rachel concentrated on her salad, she was hoping to hear from Professor Thomas, her mentor during her botany studies in college. He supported her work, and she suspected there might be something between them if she was not his student. Rachel grabbed the phone when she saw Professor Thomas's name come up as it rang.

"Thank you for calling me back! I can't believe what is happening down here. The seaweed has been acting crazy!"

Professor Thomas laughed. "What do you mean? Seaweed is a plant. It can't act anyway at all."

"Well come down here and see for yourself if you don't believe me. It has taken over the beach, the water is almost impassable, and the texture of the seaweed is foreign. You know I have catalogued over 300 species of seaweed, and believe me, this is nothing like I have ever seen."

"Rachel, it is at least a twelve hour drive to Florida from campus, but I'll come if I can. I know you well enough that you are taking this very seriously. What about your three friends?"

"None of them are interested in plant biology, so to them the seaweed is just a pain in the neck. But I really think this may be a whole new species. You have got to come and see this. I have samples, but seeing this live is awesome."

"Okay, I'll try. But no promises."

"Thanks professor." After giving him directions, she disconnected, and turned to find Darcy, Robbie and Todd watching her intently.

"What?"

"Does someone have a crush on her hot professor?" asked Darcy.

"Of course not!" Rachel exclaimed. But she felt the flush creeping up her neck and face. "I think I need some fresh air!" *Maybe they're right. Maybe this seaweed is not that special. Maybe I am just looking for an excuse to get Mark, I mean Professor Thomas to come down here.*

"No!" she said out loud. "This is an important discovery, and I want validation." To change the subject she added, "You know what? This seaweed salad is awful. Let's walk down the road to that little Italian restaurant in town and get some beer and pizza."

The others enthusiastically agreed, and the next few hours were spent discussing their trip and how to spend the rest of the evening.

"Right now I need some sleep," said Rachel. "You guys can party tonight, but I need my brain focused first thing in the morning. Don't forget we need to be up and on the water early before it gets too hot."

"Okay Mom," said Darcy. "You go home and get some rest. I'm going to enjoy this vacation. After all, we only have three days and then it's back to the books. I plan to make the most of this time off."

Rachel knew Darcy was right, they should have some fun. But she was too involved with her project to mess it up by having a hangover. She really needed to focus so she would not miss any clues as to the origin of this strange and vibrant seaweed.

Early the next morning, Rachel was the first one up. She put on coffee and some bacon, hoping to entice the others out of bed. One by one they stumbled out of the bedrooms, grumbling at the early hour.

"My head hurts. I think I drank too much," said Todd.

"Hey, it's not my fault you stayed up all night drinking," Darcy said. "Rachel, you missed a great time, by the way. We went to this crazy Karaoke bar and, after a few drinks, Todd and Robbie could not stop singing. Really funny!"

"Come on guys. Don't forget why we came here. I need to get this project completed," said Rachel. "I have our lunches already packed so we can leave right after breakfast."

"This project is why **you** came here." said Darcy. "I would just as soon sleep in today, instead of kayaking through mud and seaweed."

"We have the Kayaks for two more days Darcy, so we might as well enjoy the water. I've thought of a few more things we can do over at the island," said Robbie.

Once back out at the beach, Rachel and her friends discovered the seaweed was even thicker on the shore today, and seemed to extend out further in the water than the day before. Rachel could swear the seaweed was pulsating.

"Hey everyone! Come here and walk on this stuff. It's hot and seems to almost have a heartbeat. And the colors change from green to blue and back. Very weird!"

While her friends found the seaweed repulsive, Rachel found it beautiful.

"I think we'll pass," said Robbie. "Let's just try to reach the island while there is some water left. This seaweed is disgusting and seems to be spreading fast."

Struggling to get the kayaks in the water, Darcy, Robbie and Todd set off for the island ahead of Rachel. She was still getting samples. She remembered how the seaweed on the beach always dried out once it was out of the water, and she could not understand why this particular seaweed stayed so moist. Rachel called Professor Thomas again to let him know they were leaving Sunset Beach and heading for the island, just in case he was on his way down. She left a message on his cell phone giving him directions from Alternate Route 19 to the beach and told him she hoped he was already headed to Florida.

Looking around the beach, Rachel noticed there were hardly any tourists on the beach, and no one was in the water, highly unusual for this time of year. A few people were milling around and taking pictures of the bizarre seaweed with their cameras and cell phones.

Once Rachel caught up with her friends, she realized there was seaweed almost as far as the eye could see. It seemed to be following the kayaks and getting thicker almost as if it was trying to prevent them from getting to the island. At one point they were almost stalled.

"Okay, this is ridiculous," said Todd. "I know how much this means to you, Rachel. But I am calling off this trip. We can go back to the mainland and plan other things for the rest of our time in Florida. I am sure you have enough samples and I, for one, have seen enough of this disgusting stuff for a lifetime."

The others agreed and tried to turn the kayaks, which proved difficult. Even Rachel was getting worried and decided, as a precaution, to put in a 911 call to the Tarpon Springs police, requesting they send someone to the beach to keep people out of the water, as well as contact the area Coast Guard, thinking they might get stuck on the water and would need to be rescued. No longer obsessed with discovering a new species of seaweed, she was more afraid for their safety. The dispatcher listened patiently to Rachel's request, but expressed some skepticism that they were being surrounded by seaweed which was holding them captive on the water.

"Just send help, please! We are in trouble!"

So intent was Rachel on turning around her kayak, she failed to notice Darcy was in danger until she heard her friend scream. The seaweed was creeping up the side of Darcy's kayak and was reaching for her thigh. Darcy was backing up and trying to get away from its tentacles. Her frantic movement caused the kayak to tip sideways and Darcy fell into the water, which now seemed alive with movement, as if the seaweed had turned into pulsating iridescent snakes. Darcy disappeared.

"No," screamed Rachel, as Robbie went into the water after Darcy. She watched in horror as the seaweed seemed to swallow him up in the same area where Darcy went down. Rachel and Todd frantically paddled over to the spot where they last saw their friends, but they were nowhere to be seen. No bubbles surfaced to show that they had even been there, that they were alive somewhere below the surface struggling to breathe. The two empty kayaks were now covered by the slimy strands and were slowly sinking.

Rachel was sobbing in horror, and Todd reached over the water to hold her. The shoreline seemed miles away, and Rachel and Todd both knew they needed to get back to the mainland. Desperately paddling towards the shore, their progress was slowed by the long strands of seaweed that only seemed to grow thicker by the minute. Rachel was paddling so frantically she did not notice she was now separated from Todd by at least six feet. The seaweed wrapped itself around one of the orange fiberglass blades of Todd's paddle, slithering across the smooth wet surface towards the shaft. Todd could feel his paddle being pulled into the water, and he struggled to hold on. Long strands of seaweed were wrapping themselves around to bow of his kayak, gliding soundlessly towards his legs. Spellbound, he watched them getting closer and closer. Rachel tried to paddle towards him, hoping to pull him into her kayak, but the seaweed, once again pulsating in the gulf waters, stalled her movement.

The seaweed grabbed Todd's left sneaker. Todd desperately pulled himself free of the shoe as the seaweed covered it and pulled it towards the water.

"What do you want?" he screamed as the seaweed came back again towards his right foot. Terrified, Todd stood up in the kayak, trying to judge the distance separating his kayak from Rachel's. *Too far to jump*, he thought, but I have to try. Rachel, sensing what Todd was about to do, tried to paddle closer, but the seaweed still kept her away. Screaming in frustration, Rachel started beating the water with her paddle, trying to make a path for Todd, should he miss the kayak when he leapt across the short distance between them.

"On my count of three, I am jumping over to your kayak. Hold out your paddle, and I will try to pull myself over," yelled Todd. But he never got the chance. His jump was short, and as soon as he hit the water's surface, the seaweed seemed to rise up and swallow him.

"Oh my God," cried Rachel, over and over. Todd was gone, and seaweed covered every inch of his kayak. In a matter of minutes, it also disappeared under the surface. Rachel was alone on the water. Covering her face with her hands she could only sob, for the loss of her friends, and the knowledge that her life was almost over.

Oddly, nothing happened. The sudden quiet caused Rachel to open her eyes and look around. The pulsating water had calmed and the seaweed had retreated from her paddle. She was afraid to move, afraid any movement would cause a repeat of the violence of the previous few minutes. Rachel sensed, rather than saw a slight shift in the seaweed. Watching closely, she saw she was correct; the seaweed was moving, this time away from her kayak. It seemed to fan out in a V formation, almost inviting her to paddle towards the point. Terrified, she did nothing. The water again started to pulsate, gently this time, rocking her kayak from front to back, urging her forward. Carefully Rachel picked up her paddle and began to propel the kayak forward through the water, paddling first on the left, and then on the right, trying to keep centered. Almost thirty yards off shore, she could only concentrate on the point of the V directly in front of her, and hope the seaweed would continue its benevolence. As she neared the mainland, Rachel saw at least fifty townspeople waiting, including some police officers. She did not care who was on shore, just so she could get there safely. Rachel still could not shake the feeling the seaweed was toying with her, waiting to drag her down into the gulf waters to join her friends. In the midst of the crowd Rachel saw Professor Thomas. Everyone was urging her forward, but she noticed no one dared to step close to the shore. No one wanted to step on the seaweed. Rachel realized she could only paddle so close to the mainland. She would have to get out of the boat and walk through the seaweed to get on shore. It still seemed to be offering her safe passageway, so she gathered her samples and tentatively put one foot over the side into the water. The seaweed made no move towards her. Sliding off the top of the kayak, Rachel was in water up to her knees. Still nothing. Professor Thomas rushed into the water to help her. The seaweed once again seemed agitated, slithering up the bank to-wards the waiting crowd.

"Go back!" she screamed. He stopped and backed up slowly. The water calmed instantly, and Rachel inched forward until she reached the seaweed amassed on the shore. Just a few more feet and Rachel was in the arms of the Professor Thomas, who pulled her away from the water.

They were immediately surrounded by bystanders, paramedics and police, who were unsuccessfully trying to push the crowd back towards the parking lot and away from the shoreline.

Sobbing, and still clinging tightly to Professor Thomas, Rachel tried to reassure the small crowd that she was alright.

"Why do you think the seaweed spared you?" someone called out.

Shaking her head, Rachel replied, "I honestly don't know. Can this plant life actually feel, or think, or realize someone has a healthy respect for its very existence? I can't answer your question, but right now I need to make some phone calls and take the time to mourn my friends. Everyone please stay away from the water."

Even with this warning, Rachel noticed a few curiosity seekers making their way down to the water's edge. Only the new agitation in the water was keeping them back. The Coast Guard finally had arrived and was talking to the police about sending in some divers to locate the missing kayakers. Rachel sensed they would not be found.

Back in the parking lot, Rachel and Professor Thomas care-fully placed Rachel's collection of wet-stack samples in the back of Professor Thomas' Jeep.

As they climbed into Jeep's front seat, neither of them noticed the slight movement of the jars, or the pulsating plants as they drove away.

MURDER ON THE PRINTED PAGE

MURDER ON THE PRINTED PAGE

Lyla Roberts frowned as she pulled her car into the driveway of the small Cape Cod style house she bought as an investment. The house had been nothing but trouble; the lawn, the garden, the nosy neighbors. *And here comes one now!*

"Yoo hoo! Lyla dear, I am so glad you are home! I really need your help!"

Of course you do, thought Lyla.

"What do you need, Mrs. Newell?" said Lyla, a little sharper than she intended.

"Oh dear, oh dear," exclaimed Mrs. Newell, obviously close to tears. "I've locked myself out of the house again and I can't reach my son on the phone, though he would be angry if he had to come out here again to let me in the house. I'm so glad I gave you that spare key!"

Wordlessly, Lyla walked up the slight incline towards her front door, with Mrs. Newell following close behind. Her curly hair, an unnatural shade of orange, was bobbing up and down in the breeze. Her breath was coming in short gasps as the tiny, overweight woman struggled to keep up with Lyla.

"My goodness, dear, you are in such a hurry."

"I am just tired, Mrs. Newell; it's been a long day. Wait here and I'll bring you the key." Lyla quickened her pace, but noticed Mrs. Newell was still struggling to keep up. Opening her front door, Lyla reached around to the hook where the keys were hung, grabbed Mrs. Newell's key and nearly ran into her as her elderly neighbor reached Lyla's door.

"Here's your front door key, Mrs. Newell." Lyla held out the key, but Mrs. Newell did not take it.

"Could you come with me and open the door, Lyla. Sometimes it sticks."

Exasperated, Lyla started off towards Mrs. Newell's house, her neighbor once again struggling to keep up. Lyla thought, *I need to move back to the city. No one talks to you there. I really miss that!* She did not consider herself antisocial, she just preferred her own company to that of others, especially nosy, gossipy neighbors.

After opening her neighbor's door, Lyla turned and found Mrs. Newell in tears.

"What's wrong?" she asked, knowing she would regret the question.

"Could you just stay a little while with me? Maybe have a nice cup of herbal tea?"

Lyla pointedly looked at her watch and sighed. "Ok, but just for a little while."

An hour later, after listening to all the latest gossip about her neighbors, Lyla managed to get away from Mrs. Newell. Kicking off her shoes as she entered her front door, Lyla decided to skip dinner. She was now too tired to cook, and full of warm tea and sugar cookies. This was going to have to stop. Mrs. Newell managed to lock herself out of her house two to three times a week now, and Lyla was sure this was just an excuse to have company. On Saturdays she had to park her car in the garage and hide in her house. Pretending she was not home was the only way she was able to have some solitude. Most of the neighbors had learned to avoid Mrs. Newell, and Lyla knew she would have to do something drastic. She would have to kill her. Again.

With her job as a freelance writer for a women's magazine, Lyla was able to kill, maim, or embarrass anyone who had ever offended her. Changing their names to protect the guilty, Lyla vented her frustrations in short stories or poems. This was usually satisfying enough. Mrs. Newell was a more serious problem; she just would not go away. Lyla had run her over with a bus in a short story called, *Look Both Ways.* A poem called, *Death of a Neighbor,* had dispatched her with a heart attack. Tonight she would sit at her computer and possibly drown her in a boating accident. Then Lyla remembered her editor had called her into his office the other day and suggested she might try to write a lighter piece.

"Women like to read about romance," he told her.

She wanted to try, really, but Mrs. Newell was the thorn in her side she needed to remove. Lyla stared at her computer screen and realized she had typed, *Mrs. Newell Must Die!*" Exhaling a noisy breath, she deleted the title, but nothing else came to mind, certainly nothing "romantic". After pulling her dark hair up into a pony tail and changing into a nightshirt, Lily gave up the thought of writing for the evening. But exhausted as she was, she could not go to sleep. Knowing she was becoming obsessed, Lyla decided to take a drastic step; she would kill Mrs. Newell for real. With that thought in her mind, she was able to drift off to a dreamless sleep.

Waking refreshed the next morning, Lyla was almost cheerful as she made coffee. All she needed was a plan. *Think Lyla, think,* she admonished herself, and lost in thought she almost missed the light tapping at her back door. *Oh no. Not this early!*

Lyla could see the orange curls just peeking above the window in her back door. Gone was her good mood as she opened the back door to the smiling old lady.

"Good morning, dear. To thank you for your kindness yesterday, I baked you this coffee cake this morning. Do you mind if I come in for coffee."

"Mrs. Newell, you know I have to be at the office by nine, and I have not even showered yet."

Obviously disappointed, Mrs. Newell handed Lyla the coffee cake, which was still warm and smelled delicious. Then, her face brightening, she asked, "What time are you getting home? I'm making soup and will have it ready for you so you won't have to cook."

Lyla felt like screaming. All she wanted was to be left alone, and now she would have to stay longer in the city tonight to kill some time, just to avoid another encounter with Mrs. Newell.

"I'll be home late. Please don't bother."

She managed to push Mrs. Newell out the door, and glancing at her watch, realized she would really have to rush if she was going to be on-time for work.

Thirty minutes later, as Lyla started backing out of her driveway, she heard a tapping sound on her car window. Mrs. Newell. Of course.

"Call me if you are going to be home early Lyla. I just heard the best gossip from Mr. Stone across the street."

Lyla watched as Mrs. Newell started back down the driveway. Ignoring the fact that Lyla could not back up as long as she was waddling down the driveway in back of Lyla's car, Mrs. Newell was taking her time. *Good Lord. She is even pausing to wave at Mr. Stone!*

With murderous thoughts, Lyla put the car in reverse and stepped lightly on the gas pedal. The car slowly inched backward, but Mrs. Newell was oblivious. *Just a few feet more and she will be gone. It will be an accident.* Lyla pressed harder on the gas pedal and the car picked up speed.

"Stop, Stop!" yelled Mr. Stone from across the street. He ran over and pushed Mrs. Newell out of the way.

So close, thought Lyla. Mr. Stone was another nosy neighbor. Lyla would have to pretend she had not seen Mrs. Newell. She could not have the neighbors thinking she would actually harm the old lady. *Heaven forbid!*

Lyla jumped out of the car and ran towards Mr. Stone and Mrs. Newell, doing her best to look upset, a true emotion since her plan had failed. She reached the back of her car and saw Mr. Stone comforting Mrs. Newell, who was crying and shaking.

"I know you didn't see me, dear," said Mrs. Newell, now starting to hiccup.

Mr. Stone just glared at Lyla.

Great! I've missed my chance.

That was not Lyla's last thought as she realized too late the car was still in reverse. Unable to get out of the way, the small sedan knocked her down and ran her over, finally coming to a stop as the front tires pinned her to the ground. No, Lyla's last thought was, *I'm not the one who's supposed to die!*

But she did.

SENIOR DETECTIVE AGENCY

SENIOR DETECTIVE AGENCY

Some people think I am just a harmless old lady. Hannah Poole, obsolete at seventy years of age. That sometimes works to my advantage; one of the perks of getting older, I guess. Rattling around in my five-room Riverside Drive Apartment, just fresh into retirement, I found myself looking at the Want Ads. I must be able to do something more fulfilling than that nine to five job that bored me for so many years. An ad for a private eye caught my eye. Wouldn't that be fun?

Six months later the study of my apartment was set up as my office. *Senior Detective Agency* has been quite popular with the older crowd, and where I was once a fish out of water among the younger, more aggressive private eyes, I am now comfortable with my aging clientele.

No job is too small, so I might spend an entire day trying to discover the whereabouts of a lost cat. A cat does not leave too may clues, so finding one is harder than you think. Mrs. Silver was sure someone had stolen her large Tuxedo cat, Bosco, as she swore he never, ever left the house. Mrs. Silver mentioned that Bosco spent a lot of time watching the birds perched outside the apartment's second story window in a large maple tree, so checking out that window was my first priority. Apparently Bosco had discovered a small tear in the screen of one of the windows, made it a little bigger, and squeezed his chubby body through. After landing on a branch, two stories up, Bosco just could not get back in the window, and he was too scared to jump to the ground. Thank goodness the nice fireman I called was able to use the firetruck's ladder to reach Bosco. With a stern warning to "check the condition of all of the screens in the apartment", Bosco was safely returned to his owner.

⇒╫ ╫⇐

One favorite job was locating the lid to Mrs. Levine's lettuce crisper. She owned the crisper for at least twenty years and had become almost obsessively attached to it, even planning to leave it to her daughter when she died. She told me it had been added as an addendum to her Last Will and Testament, with other "valuables" and she really did not want to make another trip to her attorney's office to make a change. I must have looked incredulous, so Mrs. Levine patiently explained, "You know you can only get these wonderful lettuce crispers at a home party, don't you?"

I did not know that, but I do now. Once Mrs. Levine gave me the list of all her friends who had brought dishes of food to her husband Tom's retirement party, it was just a matter of a few phone calls to locate the lid. Apparently Miss Lola put it on one of her bowls by mistake and took it home with her when she left. Of course Mrs. Levine found that story ridiculous and decided to unfriend Miss Lola on Facebook.

"You never know who to trust," declared Mrs. Levine.

≕╬╪═

Last week Eleanor Potts, a well-dressed woman in her mid-seventies, came by my office. Looking around nervously, she asked me to check on the whereabouts of her husband, Harold. She stated he disappeared at least two, sometimes three afternoons a week, and when questioned, he gave no reasonable explanation. She was worried he was having an affair.

"Have you considered following him?" I asked.

"Of course not! That's why I want to hire you! What would the ladies of my church circle think if I was skulking around after my husband?"

I had to admit, it was not a pretty picture.

"I will try to find out what he has been up to," I promised. "Please let me know the next time he is ready to leave your apartment, and I will come over immediately."

Eleanor gave me her address and stated she would call when she thought Harold was getting ready to go out.

"If he is following the same pattern as the last few weeks, you can expect a call on Wednesday morning."

Sure enough, the next Wednesday morning Eleanor called and stated Harold was getting dressed in the upstairs bedroom; I went right over. Following Harold was not a problem. He left the apartment, walking slowly with a cane, and got into an older model Blue Ford Taurus. He drove almost as slowly as he walked, and had trouble staying in his own lane. I could see him weaving back and forth from my position a few car lengths back.

"Ahh, I should have guessed." Harold was headed towards the Queen's Midtown Tunnel, and if I was correct, he would drive to the Long Island Expressway, go East on the Cross Island Parkway and south to Belmont Park. Harold was a gambler! After what seemed like hours Harold slowly pulled into the large parking lot at Belmont Park. Once my car was parked a row away from Harold's car, I got out and followed him inside. He sat alone track-side, coming in occasionally to place a bet. While I was there I took a moment to place a five dollar show bet on "Sunday's Girl", who unfortunately placed sixth.

Satisfied that Harold was not having an affair, I drove back to Eleanor's apartment to give her my findings. She was unhappy about Harold's secret gambling, but relieved he was not having an affair. I also mentioned Harold's erratic driving which had me worried! Knowing Eleanor would gladly pay my fee for solving this mystery, which included gas and mileage, I decided to bill an extra five dollars for a losing show bet placed as part of my cover.

⇥ ⇤

Just this morning I met with Gladys Anderson, who presented me with a unique problem, much more complicated than lost cats, plastic lids or wandering husbands.

"Mrs. Poole, you have to help me," she begged. "My nephew is robbing me blind."

"What has he stolen?" I gently asked, hoping to stop the flow of tears. It was no use, she just cried harder, and louder. Patiently I handed her a box of tissues. When the sobbing subsided, I coaxed her into speaking again, and finishing the story.

"Well," she said, "Eddie has stolen the diamond ring my dead husband gave me on our Fifth anniversary. It must be found before Eddie can sell it for drug money."

"What makes you think Eddie is buying drugs?"

"I don't know. Why else would he need money?"

"Does he have any outstanding debts? Maybe he is trying to pay off someone. Does he gamble?"

"I don't know. I just don't know. He used to, but I thought those days were past."

The tears were starting again, so I changed the subject. "I suggest we drive up to your home in Connecticut so I can meet with Eddie and check for clues." I said, and she agreed.

"We must hurry. If he brings my ring into the city, he will most likely pawn it. I will never see it again," Gladys continued, fighting tears. "Right now I have my maintenance man, Willie, watching his every move and so far Eddie has not left the house."

On the way to Connecticut, Gladys told me some facts about her nephew, how he had been in and out of trouble since his parent's divorce. Her sister Iris had hoped he was on a better path when he married, but he often gambled away the rent money and was always looking for the next "sure thing". Finally his wife, a "wonderful girl", Gladys boasted, left him, to no one's surprise.

When we arrived at Gladys' home, there were police cars all around. Officer O'Toole, apparently the officer in charge, blocked us from entering the house, and informed Gladys her nephew was dead inside. Willie, the maintenance man, was lying on the ground with a large gash on his forehead. I stood back and listened. Walking over to the maintenance man, who was now being helped to his feet, I could not help but notice the left sleeve of his uniform was wet, unusual since there was no water nearby, and the rest of his uniform was dry.

Willie claimed Eddie had an accomplice, a gambling buddy named Jeff, and he had confronted both of them about the thefts. Jeff became violent and as they fought, Jeff's Smith and Wesson went off, mortally wounding Eddie. While attempting to get away, Jeff shoved Willie into the fireplace mantle, causing the nasty wound on Willie's forehead. Willie stated Jeff ran out of the house, and he was only able to stagger a few feet into the yard trying to catch Jeff before he collapsed. A neighbor had heard the shots and called the police.

No one was paying attention to me, so I starting walking around the property, looking for possible clues. Towards the back of the property, I saw an old well and went to examine it more closely. Looking inside I noticed a bucket hanging over the side.

"Officer O'Toole", I called. "Could you please come here for a moment?"

Obviously annoyed by the interruption from an old lady, he nevertheless came over and I showed him the bucket hanging in the well, with a small plastic bag inside. He pulled on rubber gloves and raised the bucket with a pulley. Lo and behold, the diamond ring was in the bucket. That explained the sleeve on Willie's uniform, which had obviously gotten wet when he reached into the well to place the ring the bucket.

When Willie saw us coming back from the well, carrying the small plastic bag, he started to run. Officer O'Toole was faster and had Willie down on the ground with cuffs on his wrists before Willie was able to escape. Sobbing, Willie blurted out a confession; he was the one stealing from Gladys. When Eddie discovered what he was doing, he demanded Willie cut him in on any money he was able to get from Gladys' jewelry. Neither man had counted on Gladys discovering the thefts. Willie and Eddie's scheme was perfect, except for the theft of this last ring, as it was her favorite. Eddie panicked and threatened to call the cops and blame everything on Willie, who knew he had to get rid of the only witness who could tie him to the thefts. He had a criminal record already for petty theft and would be put away for a few years if he got into trouble again. Willie was not going to let that happen.

"Oh Eddie, I have been so wrong," sobbed Gladys.

"Not so fast Ma'am," said Officer O'Toole. "From what your maintenance man, Willie, told me, I believe they were working together. I suspect the gun may be hidden around here somewhere, and when we find it, we'll check for prints to see if there are any from this "Jeff", if he even exists. If the gun is registered, we'll find the actual owner, possibly Willie. We'll also have to do some digging and check out pawn shops before we unearth the entire truth.

"If they were working together, my Eddie must have been coerced! I am just happy to have my ring back. Oh dear, what will I tell Iris, Eddie's mother?" Gladys said, tears forming in her eyes once again. "She's my younger sister and asked me if Eddie could stay with me for the summer since he was newly divorced and out of work."

"Gladys, none of this was your fault. Eddie was a grown man who made a seriously bad choice," I told her. I hugged her once before I left and promised to forward an invoice for my services.

Another mystery solved!

MIMICS

MIMICS

Something was wrong with Molly. Or maybe wrong was too strong a word; different might be a better description. Laura's bratty younger sister seemed nicer somehow. She was not following Laura and her friends around when they came over, whining to be included, and telling Mom when she was chased her away. The four year age difference between the two sisters was just too great for them to hang out together. Lately though, Molly seemed different. Quiet, poised and thoughtful. Adjectives Laura never would have applied to her before. The change was nice, if not a little unsettling. Laura's friends did not even mind Molly hanging out. When Laura thought back, the transformation seemed to begin right around the night of the party her parents threw for her sixteenth birthday.

>═╬ ╬═<

The afternoon of Laura's sixteenth birthday party, Kyle called and asked if he could stop over a few hours before everyone arrived.

He was all excited about the gift he planned to give to Laura, and wanted her to open it separate from all the other gifts.

"I know your party is not until 7:00 o'clock, but I really want to give you your gift. It's not every day you turn sixteen," he said solemnly, "so this gift is special and something you really wanted."

"What did you get me, Kyle?" Laura asked.

"You will have to wait and see."

"In that case, come on over whenever you want. Molly and I are the only ones home right now, but my parents should be back before you arrive. They went out to pick up my birthday cake and the deli platters they ordered for the party."

Kyle arrived about five o'clock, and after ringing the doorbell, he stood on the front stoop with a medium sized box in his hand and a big grin on his face. Laura opened the polished oak door and knew right away it was not the gold bracelet she had hoped for, but did her best to hide her disappointment. Kyle's dark hair curled just over the collar of his shirt and Laura thought again how handsome he was, and knew her friends thought she was lucky. Laura's hair was long and just a shade darker than blond, which complemented her dark eyes. Kyle was crazy about her. After a year of dating, they still enjoyed being around each other all the time. Laura already was thinking they would get married someday, but her mother cautioned her they were much too young to even consider such a thing. Laura was sure her mother was wrong as she doodled his name on her notebooks, linked with hers and surrounded by a heart. Nothing bad was going to happen to them. Right?

By the look on Kyle's face, Laura knew the present had to be something special, even if it was not a bracelet. He was a good boyfriend and always went out of his way to spoil her. Molly, on the other hand, was glad it was not a gold bracelet. Laura had enough jewelry that she was always flaunting in front of her friends. She secretly hoped it was something awful that Laura would hate. As soon as she had that thought Molly felt ashamed. *Was she jealous?*

She hoped not, but it was not easy being Laura's younger sister, not as pretty, and still wearing the braces she hoped would come off soon.

After Kyle handed Laura the box, she wasted no time tearing off the wrapping paper.

"OMG, *Mimics*. I love this game. Julie has it and we play it all the time. How did you know I wanted this?" Laura asked.

"What? Are you kidding? You talk about it constantly!"

"I do not. Well, maybe I do. Anyway, let's load it into the computer. We can play this before everyone comes."

Laura led Kyle over to the computer, which was on a desk just off the kitchen. She pushed her school books aside to give them more room on the polished mahogany desktop, and then she sat down to load the program. Molly came over to watch. Inquisitive at twelve, she wanted to do everything Laura did.

"What is it, Molly?" asked Laura.

"What game did you bring, Kyle?" asked Molly, ignoring her sister. She did have a small crush on Kyle and loved when he paid attention to her.

"Hey Molly. It's called *Mimics*. When we get it loaded in, I'll show you how it works."

Even though he knew Laura and Molly did not get along, he had a fondness for Laura's younger sister. With her curly dark hair and big blue eyes, Kyle knew Molly was going to be a real beauty when she grew up. He just wished Laura would treat her a little better.

"Sure Molly," Laura said, with a scowl on her face. "We'll let you watch."

Laura's mother overheard the exchange.

"Let's not ruin your birthday," she warned.

Finally the program was loaded in and **MIMICS** appeared on the screen, in large green letters. Kyle, Molly, Laura and her parents all gathered around the computer screen.

"This is so neat," exclaimed Laura. "Wait until you see what you can do. You can program in a female or male person, and make them short, tall, fat, skinny, and any race you choose. You pick it all, including the clothes, facial features, and the hair – long or short, and whatever color you want. When you are done, the person on the screen can actually look like you. That's why it's called *Mimics*, it imitates everything about you, but you control it. We play this all the time at Julie's. I wonder what I would look like with red hair."

"Can I play?" asked Molly.

"Not now. It's my birthday and my friends are coming over and they will all want to play. Maybe I will let you try it tomorrow."

The party was a great success. Three of Laura's friends, including Julie, Bella, and Kelsey, came over with their boyfriends. Unfortunately for Laura's parents, the kids all seemed to like rap music, and the pounding noise was giving them headaches. They were amazed at how much food and soda these young adults could consume, and after the cold cut platters, the chips and cake were eaten, some of the kids were raiding the upstairs refrigerator. They were like locusts!

All the girls loved to play *Mimics*. Mostly they brought up versions of themselves, but sometimes they brought up people they did not like, and made them fatter, or balding, or just ugly with exaggerated facial features.

"Look at this big nose on Amanda," said Bella. "Too bad I could not give her pimples."

"Let's make her bleached blond hair even frizzier," said Kelsey, causing a ripple of laughter amongst the girls.

"Wow, you girls are tough," said Kyle. "I hope you don't talk about the guys like this when we are not around."

Molly just watched and listened from across the room, careful not to get in Laura's way. She was allowed at the party, but she was told to stay in the background. Molly hated being the younger sister. All she wanted to do was play *Mimics*, probably because she was told she was not allowed to play. Don't you always want to do the one thing you are not allowed to do?

Later that night, after she was sure everyone had gone to sleep, Molly crept down the staircase, grateful for the carpeting that muffled any noise. Molly worked her way over to the computer on the mahogany desk. By the time the party ended, and the mess Laura's friends made cleaned up, it was well past midnight. Molly worked hard to stay awake, but this was going to be worth it; Laura would never know she had been there.

What was that noise? I hear people talking! Molly looked around in an attempt to find the voices. Could that sound be coming from the computer?

"Why are these kids so mean to each other," a female voice asked, and continued, "They say nasty things and make fun of each other's hair and clothing. How did you like the awful outfit they put on me tonight? If that skirt was any shorter, they could have just left it off! A see through blouse? How tacky was that. Those five inch heels made me look like a street walker. Those girls had the nerve to brag about their fashion sense! What about your outfit, Monica?"

"As you can see, Grace, I am unfortunately still wearing it. Silver skinny jeans, lace top and stiletto heels; I can hardly move! They could have at least put me in pajamas before shutting down the computer."

"Well," said Grace. "We turned the computer back on, didn't we? Let's shock everyone and change our clothes."

"I don't think we are supposed to do that."

"Don't be such a spoilsport Monica. We can change back before morning. I wish they had let the little one play."

"Yeah, Molly seemed pretty nice."

"And pretty, too!" said a male voice.

"Too young for you, Ted," said Monica.

They all laughed and Molly gasped in surprise. *They knew her name!*

"What was that?" asked Monica. "Is someone there? Come around to the front of the computer so we can see you."

Slowly Molly walked around the desk until she was standing directly in front of the computer screen.

"Hello," she said shyly, a shiver of fear running through her body.

"Oh, you're the little one, Molly, aren't you? Why are you coming here in the middle of the night? Shouldn't you be asleep?" Monica asked.

"This might be the only time I can play *Mimics*. Laura said she would let me play tomorrow, but I don't believe her."

"We'll let you play," called a small chorus of voices. "We'll show you exactly how it works so you can be better than everyone. First, hold out your hand and touch the screen."

⚞ ⚟

"Hey Molly," called Laura. "Come here and I'll let you play *Mimics*. I did promise you, if you remember. But you can only stay on for a little while because Kyle is coming over later."

"I'm a little busy now, Laura. Maybe I'll play after Kyle leaves."

"Are you mad at me? I know I gave you a hard time yesterday, but it was my birthday, and my game, and my friends, and well, you know. You just always can't be involved."

"I still don't want to play now."

Laura leaned in to study the screen. That one girl looked a lot like Molly, though not as animated. And best of all, she thought, this one could not talk back! Wait a minute, that girl looked exactly like Molly. How did that happen? But there was something about the eyes; they seemed to be pleading with her, and was that a small tear sliding down her left cheek?

"No. Don't be ridiculous," Laura said out loud. "Molly, come here, you've got to see this."

Molly came over and casually studied the computer screen.

"She really does look like me. Which one of your friends created a Mimic in my image?"

"I don't remember anyone doing that," answered Laura. Staring suspiciously at Molly, Laura asked, "Have you been playing on my computer? Mom, I think Molly used my computer without asking!"

"Well maybe I did play the game once or twice. I discovered something you should see, Laura. But not right now. Tonight when Mom and Dad are asleep I will show you the most interesting phenomenon."

"Why can't you show me now?"

"Just be patient. I promise this will be worth the wait."

Laura was so focused on Molly that she neglected to watch the figures on the Mimic screen. If she had been paying attention, she might have noticed one Mimic, the one that resembled Molly, was shaking her head almost unperceivably.

Later that night, the two sisters crept downstairs after their parents were asleep, and turned on the computer. Clicking onto *Mimics*, Laura saw the same figures as before.

"So Molly, what do you want to show me?"

"Laura, the people in the computer are real, just like you and your friends. They are just trapped in the game."

"What? You don't expect me to believe that, do you?"

"Of course I do. That's where I lived before I convinced Molly to change places with me."

For the first time, Laura really looked at her sister. There was something too perfect about her face. And her eyes, they looked almost transparent, devoid of emotion. Glancing back at the Molly mimic on the screen, she saw the desperation on her sister's face.

"Oh my God," Laura screamed. "Molly is inside the computer."

She felt a shove towards the computer screen, and before she could break her fall, she sensed she was being pulled into the game. Landing inside at the feet of her sister, she looked up in horror. Both sisters could only look on helplessly as outside the screen, standing beside the polished Mahogany desk, were the two Mimics, looking identical to Laura and Molly, with smug looks on their faces.

"No," screamed Laura and Molly, at the same time. Too late. A hand reached out and pushed the button on the screen, turning off the computer. Laura and Molly were left in the dark.

Molly and Laura's parents were grateful their daughters never gave them a moment's worry, though at times it did seem a little unnatural they no longer argued. Only late at night, when the house was quiet, did any doubts surface. It was only then, as they drifted off to sleep that Molly and Laura's parents thought they heard distant voices, and the sound of someone far away crying out for help.

On the other hand, the two Mimics, who now called themselves Molly and Laura, continued to live happily in their borrowed lives. Pleased to be free of the game, and careful never to play *Mimics* again.

THE TRUTH ABOUT SEA GATE ISLAND

THE TRUTH ABOUT SEA GATE ISLAND

The ferry was gone. Darn! Lilly James had overslept and was already running late when Mrs. Anderson from the condo next door stopped her just as she was about to get into her car.

"Was tomorrow garbage day, or was it re-cycling? Did you just get new patio furniture? Did you hear old Mrs. Patterson died?" On and on, no matter how many times Lilly checked her watch, or tried to explain to Mrs. Anderson that she needed to catch the last morning ferry off the island.

Now what could she do? Well first things first; a phone call to her boss, Todd Pierson. He was going to be furious. A hyper little man at best, he had called her three times last night to emphasize the importance of this meeting, each time just as she was drifting off to sleep. No wonder she had overslept this morning! Todd and Lilly had worked for the last two months on a real estate presentation to be given to the Board of Trustees regarding the long-closed

Meyer Department Store location. Todd wanted to turn the building into condos for low income families. A competing bidder wanted to tear it down and build an expensive high rise.

Lilly held the phone away from her ear as Todd screamed obscenities. She did not take it personally as she knew that Todd was justifiably angry and frustrated.

"Yes," she said. She did remember that he had asked her stay in town, but wanted the escape of her quiet island retreat.

"Now I am going to have to present this alone and we both know you are the better speaker," he fumed. And then he hung up. Loudly.

Lilly had three and a half hours to kill before the next ferry, so she decided to walk through town as she had not done in what seemed like ages. She had forgotten how pretty Sea Gate Island was, with its small shops and quiet harbor. During certain times of the year the winding streets were teeming with tourists, but now, in early fall, only the locals seemed to be left to browse through the town. The real estate presentation had taken up too much of her time for far too long, so she had not been able to enjoy this lovely island. Adjusting her expensive red leather cross-body bag, Lilly strolled in the direction of downtown, a slight breeze ruffling her shoulder length auburn hair. Oblivious to the admiring glances of a group of construction workers, Lilly was just enjoying this free morning. She wished she was wearing more sensible shoes than her new pumps with the four inch wedge heels! Walking into the first shop she came upon, Lilly noticed with pleasure it was a book shop, with racks and racks of new books out front, and older editions towards the back. The name on the sign outside the store was, "The Old Book Shop", and the musty smell supported the moniker. The store clerk, a woman Lilly judged to be in her early sixties, nodded at her, smiled, then offered her a cup of coffee, which Lilly gratefully accepted. Noticing the clerk's name tag, Lilly said,

"Thanks Helen," as Helen also offered her a pastry which Lilly hoped was from the Sea Gate Bakery, which had the reputation of excellent baked goods.

After a few moments, the clerk approached her again and said, "I know I am being forward, but I was wondering if you are employed. Since you are here in the middle of the day, I thought maybe you needed a job."

"Why, is one available?" Lilly asked, surprised by the odd question.

"Oh thank goodness," said the clerk. "I have to go out of town and can't leave the store unattended. Here are the keys, we close at six, and the instructions for the cash register, ordering and general rules for the shop are up front. Mr. Hunter stops in once a week, on Mondays, to check on you. Good luck!"

An astonished and speechless Lilly was left holding the keys to the shop as she watched the clerk run out of the store with a look of terror on her face.

"Now what?" she wondered out loud.

Well obviously she could not accept a position in a book shop on a remote island when she already had a lucrative real estate job in the city. Lord, she better call Todd to see how the meeting went this morning. Twice the call went straight to voice mail. On the third try, Todd picked up the phone, and tersely said, "Why are you calling?"

"What do you mean why am I calling? I wanted to hear about this morning's meeting with the Board of Trustees. Did they accept your offer?"

"Nice of you to care about it now, Lilly."

"Oh, don't be ridiculous, Todd. Of course I care. You know darn well I worked on that presentation just as hard as you did. We spent weeks putting in ten hour days to make sure everything was perfect. All you had to do today was present our findings to the board and convince them the condos would be a better fit for the neighborhood than an ugly, expensive high rise. So are you going to tell me or not?"

Todd paused for dramatic effect and stated, "I think we have a good shot. Mr. Foster from the Board seemed opposed to an expensive new high rise in the downtown area. The Board of Trustees will meet again privately to discuss both options. We may be asked to come in to answer questions. By the way, are you coming in at all today?"

"Well," Lilly said slowly. "There is a slight problem." She proceeded to tell Todd about the odd experience with the book shop clerk.

"You mean she just handed you the keys and left," asked an astonished Todd.

"Yes, and she really seemed to be frightened of something."

"You know this is not your problem, Lilly."

"I know, but what am I supposed to do? I can ask at some of the neighboring shops if someone knows this "Mr. Hunter", but I can't just lock the store and walk away."

"Why the heck not?"

"Oh come on, Todd. I'm not that irresponsible. It's already Thursday and Mr. Hunter is supposed to come in on Monday. I can give him the keys and be done with it. I'll be back in the office on Tuesday, in plenty of time for us to review our presentation if the Board has any questions."

"I hope so, Lilly. Your job may be on the line about this transaction."

"Well at least I already have a job, if I need one."

"Funny," Todd stated, before he hung up in her ear for the second time that day.

Lilly decided to make the best of the situation, so she kept the book shop open until noon and then visited some of the other area shops. Carly Benson, a soft-spoken young lady from the craft store next door, was decidedly vague about Helen and Mr. Hunter. Lilly got the same response at the bakery, even after Lilly praised their pastries. At the newspaper office, a Mr. Sable, a large disheveled man in a blue rumpled shirt, who was smoking a smelly cigar, claimed to have never been in the book shop, which Lilly felt was a lie as Mr. Sable refused to meet her gaze and stuttered over his reply. After several more futile attempts to get information, Lilly decided to just wait until Monday to speak with Mr. Hunter himself. Once he cleared up the mystery, she could be on her way back to the city. Or so she thought.

Friday dawned clear and cool. After spending a restless night filled with disturbing dreams, Lilly decided to just get up early and walk down to The Old Book Shop. She had time for a breakfast of coffee and a cheese pastry at the Sea Gate Bakery before heading to the shop. Deciding to not open straightaway, Lilly wandered around checking book titles and the shop's inventory. Most of the books were quite old, and Lilly suspected some were rare. A lot of the magazines were outdated and Lilly found herself thinking of the changes she would make if she owned the shop. For one thing, she would do some dusting! Every surface was covered by a thin white film, even the windows. Funny how she had not noticed this yesterday. Lilly simply got the distinct feeling of "old" as she walked around the shop. But before she did anything, Lilly decided to place another call to Todd, just to check in.

"Good morning, Todd. How is everything at the office?"

After a short pause, Todd told her the deal had fallen through. "The board called right after I opened the office to tell me they were going with the expensive high rise deal."

"I am so sorry, Todd."

"Really? By the way, you're fired!"

"What! That's ridiculous, Todd. You can't fire me over this deal. I have been with you for the last eight years. I miss one meeting and you fire me?"

"This meeting was very important to me and the finances of this company, Lilly. So yes, you are fired."

With that, Todd hung up. Lilly stood there looking at the phone in shock.

Wonderful. I just bought a condo, and now I don't have a job. Or do I? Lilly would find the answer to that question on Monday when she met with Mr. Hunter.

Friday and Saturday dragged slowly by as not one person entered the shop; not even to browse. So Lilly dusted and vacuumed. Then she washed windows. The view of the harbor was magnificent once you could see through the window panes. I wonder if Mr. Hunter will let me get rid of some of these older magazines and order more current issues, as well as new books. *I bet I could stir up some interest with a sidewalk sale! What am I thinking? I am not sure if Mr. Hunter will even keep me on. Do I even want to be here? Helen said she had to go out of town, but she may be back.*

On Monday, Lilly arrived at the book shop a few minutes before nine o'clock. She hoped Mr. Hunter would come in early so she could discuss her situation. Well, she was disappointed. It was not until the evening shadows were long upon the street, and she was about to close the book shop that Mr. Hunter put in an appearance. The brass bell attached to the front door rang for the first time that day as Mr. Hunter made his entrance. Lilly stared in fascination. Mr. Hunter was tall, dressed entirely in black down to what looked like riding boots. His dark hair was just a shade lighter than black, but it was his eyes that drew her in. They were so very pale, the lightest shade of blue she had ever seen, and she saw no humor there. Lilly put out her hand as she approached Mr. Hunter.

"Good evening sir. I am Lilly James."

"I know who you are," replied Mr. Hunter, as he drew her hand to his lips, giving her the impression he was trying to get a sense of her. How odd!

"Helen's abrupt departure would have left me in the lurch, but she assured me she had hired you as her replacement."

"She did no such thing," exclaimed Lilly.

"Yet here you are holding the keys. I see you have been busy; the book shop looks lovely."

"Thank you. I needed to keep busy until you arrived. Let me make this clear. Helen just thrust the keys at me and ran out the front door. I already had a job and would not have taken a job here."

"I understand you have been fired from your real estate job and are available to take the job as the shop's manager."

"How would you know that?"

"I make it my business to know everything about my employees."

"I am not your employee, as I have already stated. I could have just left, Mr. Hunter. I am sure Ms. Benson from the craft shop next door would have been happy to give you the keys. Out of courtesy I wanted to speak with you about the situation."

"That's not how it works, Lilly. What a lovely name. The sound just rolls off my tongue. Lilly. Yes you will do fine."

"Mr. Hunter, I am not sure what you are talking about, but I have to catch the late ferry back to the city to see about my job."

"I am afraid that will not be possible, Lilly. I need you here," Mr. Hunter said softly.

Something in Mr. Hunter's tone sent a chill through Lilly's body. She took a step backward to create some space between them.

"This is my island," he went on. "I allow everyone to live and work here. I am your host."

"What? Like Mr. Rourke from *Fantasy Island?*"

A small smile played across Mr. Hunter's lips, just briefly. His eyes seemed to darken.

"Mr. Rourke was a fantasy. I assure you, I am not. You may only leave this Island if you bring me a replacement for the book shop, as Helen brought you. No one in town will come to your rescue. All the town residents supply my needs, and I protect and care for them in return. You were allowed to purchase your charming little condo only on my approval."

As Lilly began to protest, Mr. Hunter drew closer. His pale eyes pulled her in until Lilly could not breathe.

What on earth was happening? Thought Lilly in the brief moment before Mr. Hunter flashed beautiful white fangs that were now playing gently over Lilly's lovely long, white neck.

The rest of Monday night was a blur. Lilly was not even sure how she got home, but she woke up alone in her condo as the morning light shimmered through her window, cutting a narrow path across the bedroom's oak plank floor. Coffee. She needed hot, strong coffee. Sitting by the kitchen window sipping the strong liquid, Lilly could not make sense of what had happened the night before. A bruise on her neck told her the encounter with Mr. Hunter was not a dream. After a quick shower, Lilly dressed, and decided to check out the book shop to see if Mr. Hunter was still there. As if on autopilot, Lilly walked the short distance through town towards The Old Book Shop. The baker and Ms. Benson nodded "good morning" to her as she passed, but she barely noticed.

Lilly pondered her situation. Staying on the island might prove to be exciting because of the dashing Mr. Hunter, but her life would essentially be over, and her freedom gone. Smiling to herself she picked up the phone and made a call.

"Todd, I know you are really angry with me, but I have found a lucrative real estate deal perfect for you to handle. It might just make you forget your disappointment over losing the condo deal. Why don't you take the ferry out to the island next Monday so we can discuss it? You are really going to like Mr. Hunter. I promise he will change your life."